"Save me a waltz."

Luke's voice was suddenly deeper, and tension vibrated between them.

His words reminded Rebecca of the last time they'd waltzed together and how it felt to be held in his arms.

The need to leave her chair, to take the short two steps separating them, run her hands over the bare muscles of his chest and arms and lift her mouth to his was nearly overwhelming. The force of emotions he raised in her was disconcerting. She decided to obey the alarm bells that were screaming caution in her brain.

"I will—if you're there." Which was as noncommittal as she could be without refusing him outright. She stood. "And since it sounds as if it's going to be a long day tomorrow, I think I'll try to get some sleep." She turned toward the screen door, hesitating to say good-night, before she pulled open the door.

"Good night." His voice was hushed, quieter than usual, but it still sent shivers up her spine.

Dear Reader,

Well, it's that time of year again—and if those beautiful buds of April are any indication, you're in the mood for love! And what better way to sustain that mood than with our latest six Special Edition novels? We open the month with the latest installment of Sherryl Woods's MILLION DOLLAR DESTINIES series, *Priceless*. When a pediatric oncologist who deals with life and death on a daily basis meets a sick child's football hero, she thinks said hero can make the little boy's dreams come true. But little does she know that he can make hers a reality, as well! Don't miss this compelling story....

MERLYN COUNTY MIDWIVES continues with Maureen Child's *Forever...Again,* in which a man who doesn't believe in second chances has a change of mind—not to mention heart—when he meets the beautiful new public relations guru at the midwifery clinic. In *Cattleman's Heart* by Lois Faye Dyer, a businesswoman assigned to help a struggling rancher finds that business is the last thing on her mind when she sees the shirtless cowboy meandering toward her! And Susan Mallery's popular DESERT ROGUES are back! In *The Sheik & the Princess in Waiting,* a woman learns that the man she loved in college has two secrets: 1) he's a prince; and 2) they're married! Next, can a pregnant earthy vegetarian chef find happiness with town's resident playboy, an admitted carnivore... and father of her child? Find out in *The Best of Both Worlds* by Elissa Ambrose. And in Vivienne Wallington's *In Her Husband's Image,* a widow confronted with her late husband's twin brother is forced to decide, as she looks in the eyes of her little boy, if some secrets are worth keeping.

So enjoy the beginnings of spring, and all six of these wonderful books! And don't forget to come back next month for six new compelling reads from Silhouette Special Edition.

Happy reading!

Gail Chasan
Senior Editor

Please address questions and book requests to:
Silhouette Reader Service
U.S.: 3010 Walden Ave., P.O. Box 1325, Buffalo, NY 14269
Canadian: P.O. Box 609, Fort Erie, Ont. L2A 5X3

Cattleman's Heart

LOIS FAYE DYER

Silhouette®

SPECIAL EDITION®

Published by Silhouette Books

America's Publisher of Contemporary Romance

To Constance Martynow, a wonderful sister-in-law
and devoted fan, who welcomed me into the family
and has offered constant support over the years.
You are deeply loved, gratefully appreciated. Thank you.

 SILHOUETTE BOOKS

ISBN 0-373-24605-6

CATTLEMAN'S HEART

Copyright © 2004 by Lois Faye Dyer

Visit Silhouette at www.eHarlequin.com

Printed in U.S.A.

Books by Lois Faye Dyer

Silhouette Special Edition

Lonesome Cowboy #1038
He's Got His Daddy's Eyes #1129
The Cowboy Takes a Wife #1198
The Only Cowboy for Caitlin #1253
Cattleman's Courtship #1306
Cattleman's Bride-To-Be #1457
Practice Makes Pregnant #1569
Cattleman's Heart #1611

LOIS FAYE DYER

lives on Washington State's beautiful Puget Sound with her husband, their yellow Lab, Maggie Mae, and two eccentric cats. She loves to hear from readers and you can write to her c/o Paperbacks Plus, 1618 Bay Street, Port Orchard, WA 98366.

MONTANA

Billings

Colson •

IDAHO

WYOMING

NEVADA

San
Francisco
Bay Area

UTAH

CALIFORNIA

N

All underlined places are fictitious.

Chapter One

"I'm definitely not in California anymore."

Rebecca Parrish Wallingford turned in a slow circle, her gaze sweeping the ranch yard. She braced herself against the open door of the rental car and took in the buildings set in a neat half circle around the dusty square. Weather and time had long since stripped the paint from the two-storied ranch house until it was a uniform dark gray. A tall, gnarled maple shaded the left side of the house, its leafy branches brushing against gray wood, the second story's sashed windows and the roof of the deep porch that edged the front of the house. A matching maple sheltered the other side of the house, set back and slightly nearer the far end of the structure.

The building was silent, slumbering beneath the hot June sun. If people were within, Rebecca could neither see nor hear them.

She glanced past the house to the sprawling outbuildings on her left. New lumber and shingles created a patchwork of pale color against the weathered walls and roof of the large barn while the attached corral was constructed entirely of raw, unpainted wood. Three dusty pickup trucks stood outside a long shed just beyond the corral. The sound of hammers thudding against nails and the high-pitched scream of a saw slicing through wood broke the afternoon quiet.

A man stepped from the dim interior of the shed into the hot sunlight and strode toward the trucks.

He glanced toward the house, saw Rebecca and abruptly changed direction to angle away from the back of a truck loaded with lumber, and move toward her.

He was shirtless, a tool-hung carpenter's belt riding low on his hips, its weight dragging the waistband of faded denim jeans below his navel. A straw cowboy hat shaded his face, leather gloves on his hands. Rebecca stared, riveted by the slow saunter of long legs, the gleam of hot sunlight on sleek brown shoulders, the supple flex and shift of muscles as he moved.

"Afternoon, ma'am." He halted a few feet away. "Something I can do for you? Are you lost?"

His voice was a deep drawl. She felt the impact of

his gaze when it met hers as if he'd reached out and touched her.

Shivers feathered up Rebecca's spine and heat grew, easing its way through her body. Her black linen suit and white cotton shell, chosen for traveling in the summer heat, felt suddenly much too warm. Shocked by her reaction, she took a mental step back and desperately sought detachment.

Sweat dewed the angles and hollows of his face, dampening the ends of his hair where it curled, a shade too long, behind his ears and at his nape. Thick eyebrows, the same deep brown as his hair, arched over dark gold eyes, the sharply defined cheek-bones—fit companions to a blade of a nose that was slightly crooked. Rebecca wondered fleetingly if he'd broken it sometime in the past. His wasn't a classically handsome face but there was something so essentially male about him that Rebecca felt threatened by the raw power he exuded. At five feet eight inches tall, she rarely felt intimidated by males, but this man made her vividly aware that she was smaller boned and distinctly feminine.

Her reaction set alarm bells jangling inside her head.

And the way he was looking at her, his golden eyes hooded, hot with more than the afternoon heat, only made the alarms ring louder.

Other men had looked at her and she'd known they wanted her. She'd never felt the slightest physical reaction. Her heart hadn't pounded harder. Her skin hadn't heated. That this man could arouse a reaction with only a look was irritating beyond words.

"I hope I'm not lost. I'm looking for Jackson Rand, owner of the Rand Ranch."

His gaze sharpened, a faint frown creasing his forehead.

"I'm Jackson Rand."

Oh no. Rebecca stiffened. Her day had swiftly gone from bad to worse.

"It's a pleasure to meet you, Mr. Rand." She forced herself to step forward and extend her hand, steeling herself. His much bigger hand engulfed hers, his fingers and palm callused and hard against hers for a brief moment before he released her. "I'm Rebecca Wallingford with Bay Area Investments—I believe you're expecting me."

If Rebecca had stiffened, Jackson Rand went rigid. His gaze narrowed, swiftly flicking over Rebecca from head to toe in a swift searing assessment.

"No, I'm expecting a man named Walter Andersen."

"Walter had a minor heart attack yesterday and I've been assigned to take his place. I trust I haven't arrived at an inconvenient time?"

He stared at her for a long moment without speaking, his gaze unreadable.

"No," he said finally. "The timing isn't inconvenient, but I wasn't expecting a woman." He gestured toward the shed and barns. "We're updating the out-buildings but the house hasn't been touched and there's no room for a woman."

"I'm sure the accommodations you planned for Mr. Andersen will be perfectly fine for me, Mr. Rand. As long as I have a bed, somewhere to shower, brew a pot of tea and plug in my laptop, I'll be perfectly comfortable."

"I doubt that, lady. The house has four bedrooms and, at the moment, three of them are occupied by me and my crew. You'll be the only woman in a house full of men."

Rebecca schooled her face not to reflect her instant dismay. She'd been told that the owner of Rand Ranch would provide housing, but sharing that housing with a crew of men wasn't a possibility she'd considered. Her mind raced, considering the problem.

"Did you assign a room to Mr. Andersen or was he going to share?"

"He would have had a room to himself," Jackson said shortly.

"Then I'm afraid I don't see the problem, Mr. Rand."

"You don't? Then let me lay it out for you. Moving a woman into a house with four men for several months is asking for trouble. Lots of trouble. And I'm too damn busy to deal with it."

Rebecca struggled to ignore the quick rise of anger at his blunt comment. "I'm a professional, Mr. Rand.

I often have to work with men. I've never had a problem before and I don't expect to have one here.''

"Expect to." His frown deepened. "Hank is too old to chase you, but he flat doesn't like women and he's not going to want you around. Mick and Gib are more likely to hit on you and fight over whoever wins."

"I'm an engaged woman, Mr. Rand," Rebecca said evenly, wondering just what she was getting into. *I can always drive into Colson and look for a room if this situation becomes impossible.* But Colson was a thirty-mile drive each way, which was the reason Jackson Rand had agreed to house Walter Andersen in the first place. "And, therefore, off-limits. But if your employees don't respect my position, then I can deal with the problem."

His expression didn't change, but Rebecca didn't miss the irritation that gleamed in Jackson Rand's eyes.

"I doubt it, but I'll put a lock on your door."

She met his barely concealed frustration with a cool glance and lift of an eyebrow. "I appreciate that. Now, if you would show me where I'll be staying, Mr. Rand. I've been traveling since 5:00 a.m. It's been a long day."

For the space of a heartbeat, Jackson didn't move, his gaze unreadable. Then he seemed to reach a decision, tugged his hat lower over his forehead and nodded toward her car.

"Is your luggage in the trunk?"

"Yes."

He held out his hand. Rebecca dropped the car keys into his palm, and he strode past her to the back of the car.

Rebecca drew a deep breath and bent, stretching across the interior of the car to reach for her purse and laptop on the passenger seat. Leather bags in hand, she closed the car door and turned, halting in midmovement when she nearly bumped into Jackson.

Startled, she took a quick step back, brought up short when her back met the warm metal of the car.

Jackson didn't comment. He merely nodded toward the house, a suitcase in each hand and one tucked beneath his arm.

"After you."

Vividly aware of the man walking behind her and the ease with which he carried her heavy bags, Rebecca moved past him. A split-rail fence enclosed the expanse of cropped grass surrounding the house and a weathered gate was set into the rails to access the stone path leading to the porch steps.

The metal latch on the old gate was shiny and new, opening easily beneath her hand. She stepped through onto the stone path and paused, thinking to close the gate behind Jackson, but he gave it a nudge with his boot and the old gate swung silently closed on new, well-oiled hinges.

Rebecca moved up the path ahead of him. Accus-

tomed to the micromaintained, upscale homes in her
native San Francisco, Rebecca was fascinated by the
old house. Upon closer inspection, she realized that
one of the three wide, shallow porch steps was new
wood, obviously recently installed. The older boards
on the porch floor creaked softly beneath her feet,
Jackson's boots ringing hollowly as he followed, then
reached around her to pull open the screen door.

The room beyond was a square entry hallway with
scarred wooden floors that gave onto a stairway to the
right, an open doorway to a living room on the left,
and a hallway ahead that clearly led to the back of
the first floor.

What she could see of the old house reminded Rebecca of a friend's house undergoing restoration in
Daly City, one of the older suburbs of San Francisco.

"The bedrooms are upstairs."

Jackson's deep drawl startled Rebecca, and she
turned to follow him upstairs, trailing her hand over
the newel post and the oak banister, worn smooth and
satiny.

Five doors stood open along the hallway, a worn
runner patterned in faded pink cabbage roses filling
its length.

Jackson strode down the hall ahead of her.

"This is the bathroom. There's only one." He
barely paused as he passed the door.

Rebecca caught a quick impression of black-and-
white tiles, a pedestal sink and a huge claw-foot white

bathtub as she inhaled a heady mix of soap and male aftershave.

"You can use this bedroom." He disappeared through a door at the far end of the hall.

Rebecca paused on the threshold, swiftly scanning the room. Jackson deposited her bags at the foot of a simple, white-painted iron bedstead. An oak nightstand with a lamp centered atop its otherwise bare surface was next to the bed, and an old but solid oak dresser stood against the far wall, across from the open doors of a small closet where a cluster of empty wire hangers hung on the wooden rod. A small, square table was placed beneath the window; a straight-backed wooden chair next to it didn't match the table but looked sturdy enough.

No pictures hung on the bare walls, no curtains draped the tall, sashed window. The room held only the bare essentials but it was scrupulously clean.

"It's not fancy."

Rebecca glanced quickly at Jackson and found him watching her, arms folded across his chest.

"It's fine," she assured him, smiling slightly at his look of disbelief. "Believe me, I've stayed in much worse places. This is perfectly okay."

"If you say so."

He looked unconvinced, but shrugged and moved toward the door. He paused on the threshold, looking back at her.

"Make yourself at home. I'll be working down at

the barn until six or so, but this evening we can go over the books.''

''That sounds good,'' Rebecca agreed.

He nodded abruptly, turned on his heel and left.

Rebecca stood motionless, listening to the sound of his boots against the bare oak floors as he descended the stairs and crossed the hallway, then the squeak and slam of the screen door as he left the house.

''Well.'' She dropped onto the edge of the bed, toed off her shoes and stared blankly at the bare wall.

She wasn't sure what she'd expected from the owner of the Rand Ranch, but she definitely hadn't anticipated a man like Jackson Rand.

She'd worked for her mother's venture capital firm for the last four years, ever since she graduated from college. She'd often been assigned on-site work with various firms, requiring her to travel to the area and remain there for several weeks. This was different. When her mother, Kathleen, the head of Bay Area Investments, had asked her to fill in for a co-worker stricken with a sudden illness, she'd readily agreed. She wasn't elated to learn that the assignment called for a stay of two months, perhaps longer, on a ranch in eastern Montana, and she was puzzled by her mother's decision to loan hundreds of thousands of dollars to a rancher. Kathleen's usual investments were in high-profile business ventures and her specialty was San Francisco real estate. When she'd questioned her mother, Kathleen's response that the investment was well-researched and wise had left Rebecca debating her mother's decision-making for the first time.

More important than the puzzle of why her mother had agreed to lend money to Jackson Rand, however, was her reaction to the rancher.

Rebecca recognized the signs of physical attraction—the heat that moved through her veins when he was near, the increased pace of her heartbeat. She'd felt those same things when she'd had a crush at seventeen. The crush had ended badly and the experience had reinforced the bitter lessons hammered home by her stepfather over the years. Harold Wallingford had never let her forget that she was illegitimate, the product of a passionate liaison by her mother before she married him. Harold's too frequent comments and her unfortunate experience at seventeen had taught Rebecca a valuable lesson—that common sense went out the window when hormones took over. She'd avoided any recurrence of the madness of attraction ever since and she'd been amazingly lucky. She'd even chosen her fiancé, Steven, based on common interests and goals. No passion raged between them, and Rebecca reminded herself that she was glad his kisses generated only mild pleasure with no trace of out-of-control emotions.

She glanced down at her hand and smoothed a fingertip over the diamond solitaire. There was no reason to think that her status as an engaged woman wouldn't hold the men at the Rand Ranch at arm's length. *Especially Jackson Rand.* Because she was determined to control any impulses from her own wildly attracted hormones. *Discipline and commitment.*

That decided, Rebecca stood, stripping off her black linen suit jacket. She unzipped the pencil-straight matching skirt and padded on stockinged feet to the closet. The wire hangers weren't the best for the expensive linen, but Rebecca had long since learned to make do while traveling. She pulled the white cotton, short-sleeved shell off over her head and dropped it on the bed before swinging one of the suitcases atop the blanket-covered sheets.

There was no spread on the bed, but the corners of the blankets and sheets were folded and tucked with military preciseness. Rebecca wondered if Jackson had done a stint in the army. He'd certainly learned neatness somewhere. The small glimpses she'd caught of the house plus the appearance of her bedroom all testified that Jackson Rand was a man with a tendency toward sparse, clean, tidy surroundings.

She hoped he was as careful about his financial dealings. It would make her job over the next few months much easier. Clients who had to be reminded to be fiscally cautious were often difficult clients, and she suspected that handling Jackson Rand in any aspect wouldn't be an easy task.

Accustomed to traveling light, Rebecca unpacked with quick efficiency and tucked her empty suitcases into the back of the small closet. Then she pulled on a green silk tank top and tucked it into the waistband of a gathered cotton skirt, slid her feet into leather sandals, picked up a box of English Breakfast tea bags from the blanket-covered bed and headed back downstairs.

She felt a bit as if she were intruding but, as Jackson's home would also be her home for the next few months, she ignored the concern and walked down the hall into the kitchen.

The stripped-down tone of the rest of the house was evident in the kitchen, also, but the wide window over the sink and the back door's square glass let in cheery sunlight. There was something very welcoming and warm about the knotty-pine cupboards with their plain white counters. A square maple table and chairs took up one corner of the room and a white stove and refrigerator faced each other at opposite ends of the cabinets.

The house was nothing like the Knob Hill mansion she'd grown up in, nor the apartment she'd bought after college and where she now lived. The upscale rooms on the twentieth floor of a posh building on Van Ness Avenue, a bustling downtown location, were a planet removed from these. But the differences only made the house more interesting.

"Nothing fancy, but very functional," Rebecca murmured, her gaze slowly surveying the kitchen. A battered copper teakettle sat on a back burner of the stove. "Ah," she said with satisfaction.

It took only moments to fill the kettle with cold tap water and set it on the stove to heat. Rebecca opened cupboard doors until she found several mugs. The one she took down had a Montana State Fair and Rodeo emblem on the side. None of the cupboards held good china, although there was a collection of mismatched dishes, glasses, cups and bowls.

While she waited for the kettle to boil, she glanced at the clock and realized that it was nearly five o'clock.

Rebecca was hungry. She'd swallowed less than half of the limp chicken and dry rice served as lunch on the plane. Then she'd downed a bottle of water and a candy bar while waiting for her rental car to be processed at the airport, but except for two tall take-out coffees she drank on the drive from Billings to Colson and the bagel she'd eaten at her 6:00 a.m. meeting before leaving for the airport in San Francisco, that was the sum total of her food intake for the day.

She was beyond hungry. She was starved.

The teakettle whistled, startling her and she quickly poured boiling water into her mug.

"What the hell are you doing?"

Rebecca jumped and spun to look at the door. A man stood just outside the screen door in the utility room. He yanked open the door and stepped into the kitchen, and she got a clearer view of him. He wasn't a tall man; in fact, he was probably an inch or so shorter than her own five feet eight, but his legs were bowed and his back slightly bent, making it difficult to know how tall he might have been when young. His dusty jeans and snap-front western shirt were faded blue and worn white in places, his brown cowboy boots smeared with mud. At least, Rebecca assumed it was mud. She wasn't sure. A shock of white hair was startlingly pale against the dark, weathered tan of his lined face, and bright blue eyes watched her suspiciously.

"Well?" he demanded.

Rebecca realized that she'd been staring, speechless, at him and hadn't answered his question.

"I'm just brewing a mug of tea," she offered. He didn't relax, his gaze just as suspicious. "I'm the accountant from Bay Area Investments."

The blue gaze sharpened. "I thought the accountant was a man."

"He was. Is. He was stricken with a sudden illness, and the company sent me to take his place."

"Humph," the old man snorted. "That's ridiculous. We can't have a woman on the place."

"So Mr. Rand said," Rebecca said dryly, wondering if every man on Rand Ranch would dislike her on sight. "I'm guessing that you must be Hank?"

"That's right. How'd you know?"

"Mr. Rand mentioned that one of the four men staying here didn't care for women."

"That's right. I don't. Women are nothin' but trouble."

"I promise I'll do my best not to cause any trouble," Rebecca assured him gravely.

"Hah. Promise all you want, won't make any difference. Trouble follows women, regardless of what they say."

Rebecca could see that the conversation wasn't getting anywhere.

"I was just making a mug of tea, Mr., um, Hank. Would you like one?"

He gave her a withering glare. "No. Don't drink tea. That's a woman's drink, 'cept for iced tea loaded with sugar in the summertime."

"Oh." Rebecca bit the inside of her lip to keep from grinning. Hank reminded her of elderly Mr. Althorpe, her neighbor at her condo in San Francisco. He proclaimed long and loud that he hated women, but he was a soft touch for the double-chocolate brownies she brought him from the bakery on the next block. She wondered briefly if the bakery would give her the recipe so she could try chocolate bribery on Hank.

"Men drink coffee, beer or whiskey," the old man proclaimed, stomping to the sink. He scrubbed his hands and face, drying them on the towel hung on a rack inside the lower cabinet door.

"Would you like me to make you coffee, then?"

"No." He shot her a scathing glance. "Women never make it strong enough."

"Ah, I see." She collected her tea, tossed the tea bag in the trash, stirred in sugar and retreated to the relative safety of the table.

"If you're gonna be livin' here, you're gonna have to help with chores," Hank warned.

"Certainly. Is there a schedule?"

"Of sorts. I do most of the cookin' and everybody else helps out with cleanin' up in the kitchen and the rest of the house."

Rebecca didn't miss the pointed look Hank gave her. Clearly, the kitchen was Hank's territory.

"Can I help you with dinner tonight?" she offered, expecting him to refuse. To her surprise, he didn't.

"Since I'm runnin' late tonight, I suppose you can," he agreed grumpily.

"What can I do?" She stood.

"You can get five good-sized baking potatoes from the sack in the basement. The door to the cellar is on the back porch."

"Right." Rebecca stepped into the utility room. A washer and dryer took up half of one wall, the other half lined with coat hooks and a collection of jackets. Below them, several pairs of rubber or leather boots stood. The far wall had more hooks for jackets and the door to the back step, standing open with the screen door outside closed. To her left, cabinets lined

the wall on each side of a door. She pulled open the
door, flicked on the switch and carefully descended
steep stairs to the cool, concrete-walled basement.
Rough plank shelves lined the walls, filled with
enough canned goods to feed an army. She found the
gunny sack of potatoes leaning against the wall. Jug-
gling an armful, she left the basement for the kitchen
and crossed to the sink. Hank shot her a glance when
she tumbled the pile into the sink and began to wash
them. Without commenting, she scrubbed them clean,
deftly stabbed each three times with a knife from the
block atop the counter and slipped them into the oven,
setting the temperature at four hundred.

''Potatoes are in,'' she told Hank. ''What else can
I do?''

When Jackson opened the back door and stepped
into the utility room off the kitchen, it was nearly six-
thirty. He was hot, dirty and tired. And he still hadn't
decided what he was going to do about Rebecca Wallingford.

He saw her through the screen door to the kitchen
the minute he stepped into the utility room. She was
standing with her back to him, stirring something in
a pan on the stove. Gone was the sophisticated black
business suit and heels, replaced by a gathered white
skirt that cinched in at her narrow waist and left the
smooth, tanned length of legs bare from above her
knees. The old radio on the shelf by the back door
was tuned to a rock-and-roll station, and her ebony

ponytail swung back and forth, brushing her nape as she swayed to the music.

Emotions, basic and primitive, stirred in Jackson. He easily recognized the surge of lust in the mix. Rebecca Wallingford was a beautiful woman; he'd have to be a eunuch not to respond to her. The other reactions were more difficult to analyze. He suspected that it had something to do with coming in from work and finding a beautiful woman cooking dinner in his kitchen. The inferences to hearth and home and a woman of his own were obvious.

Oh, no. I'm not going there.

He stepped inside the kitchen and turned down the volume on the radio. Rebecca spun around, her hand flying to her heart.

"Oh, it's you. You startled me."

"Sorry." For a long moment, he couldn't look away from wide emerald eyes fringed with thick black lashes. She had a mouth that conjured up erotic fantasies, and the green tank top clung to full breasts that the suit jacket she'd worn earlier had concealed. He realized that he was staring and yanked his gaze away from her chest to glance past her at the stove. "Where's Hank?"

"He went to the basement to find canned peaches for dessert."

Behind Jackson, the sound of male voices and laughter grew louder. The back-room door slapped shut, then the inner screen door opened and two men stepped into the kitchen. They halted abruptly just inside the door and stared at Rebecca with identical expressions of surprise and interest.

"Whoa. Who's this?"

The taller of the two grinned at her, his blue eyes alive with interest on an open, friendly face beneath close-cropped blond hair. The other man was shorter, with dark brown hair and a handsome face. Rebecca instinctively liked the taller man and withheld judgment on the handsome one.

She glanced at Jackson and found him watching her reaction, eyes narrowed.

"This is the accountant. She'll be staying here for the next couple of months or so. Rebecca Wallingford," he nodded at the blond man, "this is Gib Thompson..."

"Hello." The lanky young man grinned and nodded a greeting.

"...and Mick Haworth."

"Pleased to meet you." An engaging smile wreathed Mick's handsome face.

"It's nice to meet you, too."

"Where are you from, Rebecca?" Gib asked.

"San Francisco."

"Yeah? Are you..."

"Out of the way." Hank's testy voice interrupted them. He elbowed his way past Mick and Gib and shot them a glare. "If you two want to eat tonight, you'd better get washed up. I ain't waitin' dinner on you while you stand here jawin' with Rebecca.''

The two shot Rebecca apologetic looks and left the room. Their boots sounded on the stairs, the din of their friendly arguing floating behind them down the stairway.

"You, too, boss."

Jackson left the kitchen without comment. The radio played an old Stones tune as his boots sounded on the stair treads.

By the time Jackson and the other two came back downstairs, faces, hands and arms washed free of dust and grime, Rebecca was folding napkins and tucking them under silverware. The maple table was set with mismatched china, a crockery bowl filled with salad greens and red tomatoes making a bright spot of color against the wooden tabletop. Hank forked steaks onto a platter and set it on the table.

"Well, come on, set down and eat before everything gets cold."

Chairs scraped against the wooden floor, Mick and Gib jostling each other to pull out Rebecca's chair. Jackson gave them a steely glare and they retreated to their own seats. Rebecca calmly seated herself and picked up her napkin.

For a few moments, the silence was punctuated only by requests to pass food and the scrape of spoons and forks against bowls and plates.

The quiet was broken by Gib.

"So, Rebecca, you're an accountant? In San Francisco?"

"Yes." She picked up her water glass and sipped. "I work for an investment firm downtown."

"And you do this often?" Mick asked.

Rebecca glanced up. "Do I do what often?"

"Travel to a strange place and live with strangers?"

"I travel a lot," she conceded. "But I usually stay in a hotel room by myself."

"And that doesn't bother you, traveling all the time?" Gib asked, his voice curious.

"No, not at all. I like visiting new places, meeting new people."

"And you don't miss being at home?"

Rebecca had a quick mental image of her San Francisco apartment with its few pieces of furniture and the unpacked boxes still shoved into closets after three years. Her busy traveling life left little time to build a nest. "I miss San Francisco," she admitted. "I love the city. But I rarely get homesick when I'm away. I'm usually too busy working and exploring a new city."

"So most of your jobs are in the city?" Mick asked, ignoring his half-eaten steak to stare at her.

"Until now, all of my clients have been located in medium to large cities. But that doesn't mean that our firm never has clients in smaller towns."

"But you've never worked in a small town," Jackson interjected.

"No," Rebecca admitted. She lifted an eyebrow, trying to keep annoyance from her voice. "Are you concerned about my ability to deal with a rural-based business rather than an urban corporation?"

"No." He shook his head. "I'm concerned with your ability to put up with the isolation of a ranch after living in the city."

"I have a car," she pointed out. "And Colson isn't that far away."

"True. But Colson isn't San Francisco, not even close. You're a long way from gourmet restaurants, Starbucks coffee and the opera."

"I don't go to the opera."

He shrugged. "Then, the ballet. Whatever it is that you like to do in the city, you're not likely to find here."

"Maybe not." She narrowed her eyes, determined to squelch the urge to lose her temper. "But I'm sure there are other things unique to the area and unavailable in the city that I'll find here."

He looked unconvinced. "I'm sure there are, but I doubt you'll like any of them."

Rebecca forced a small smile. "I have no doubt I'll find them fascinating. In any event, I won't be here forever. Two or three months is longer than my usual assignments but the time will pass quickly enough."

"You don't usually stay at a company for three months? Why so long this time?"

His question seemed casual, but Rebecca didn't miss the intensity with which he watched her.

"I don't know." She was suddenly aware that everyone at the table had stopped eating, their attention wholly focused on her. She chose her words carefully. "As far as I know, this is the first time Bay Area Investments has made a loan to a rancher. Perhaps the company is being cautious because this is a trial project in a new area."

"Maybe." Jackson was unconvinced. Gut instinct told him that she was holding something back. She sipped water, and her gaze met his without evasion over the rim of the glass. He didn't think she was lying, but doubted she was telling him everything she knew.

Rebecca glanced around the table. "This steak is excellent," she said politely, changing the subject without worrying about subtlety. "Is it from beef raised here on the ranch?"

Hank hooted. Jackson's mouth twisted with wry humor.

"I wish I could say yes. The few cattle left on the place when I took over were wild and tough as rawhide." He gestured at the steak on her plate. "This came from a neighbor. I traded him a side of beef for some repair work I did on his barn roof."

"So you don't raise beef? I thought I read in the report that you raised cattle?"

"I raise purebred bulls for breeding. A bull-breeding operation can be very profitable, if done right, but the start-up costs are prohibitive because of the high price of investing in good stock."

"Ah. I see." Rebecca sipped her ice water and thought about his words. "So the initial investment is high, but the return is equally high?"

"It can be. If you're lucky. And careful."

"I understand that caution is important to any business, but how is being lucky important for profit in breeding bulls?"

"Because there are a hundred problems that can keep a bull from being able to reproduce—if the owner is unlucky enough to have a sick bull, the profit is zero."

"I see." Jackson's comments brought home to Rebecca the inherent risk of investing in a business based on living animals. Once again, she wondered why her mother had gambled company money on the Rand Ranch.

"And a purebred bull can be downright touchy about procreatin'," Hank interjected. "No matter what the BSE report says, he might have problems."

"What's a BSE report?" Rebecca inquired, curious.

"It stands for Breeding Soundness Examination

and it's an exam by a vet to verify that the animal is healthy,'' Jackson explained.

"Oh.'' Rebecca wasn't sure just how much information she wanted him to explain to her about the breeding problems of bulls.

Jackson pushed back his chair and stood, gathering up his plate and utensils.

"When you're done eating, I'll show you the computer and the books.''

"I'm finished.'' She stood, too, and carried her plate and utensils to the sink.

"It's Gib and Mick's night to wash the dishes.'' Jackson took them from her. "You helped cook dinner, they'll clean.''

"All right.'' Not about to argue, Rebecca tucked a strand of hair that had escaped from her ponytail holder back behind her ear. "If you'll show me where the office is, I'll be glad to get acquainted with the computer and your bookkeeping system.''

"It's down the hall, first door on the left.''

He stood back, waiting for her to precede him, and Rebecca nodded to the others and left the room.

The office was tucked between the kitchen and the stairway; Jackson pushed the door open and stood back to let Rebecca enter. Twice the size of her bedroom, the office had two tall sashed windows without curtains, white-painted walls, an old-fashioned oak desk and a bulky leather-covered sofa and chair. She took several steps into the room and paused, diverted by the large map that took up much of the wall behind the desk. A rough wood frame edged the glass that covered the yellowed hand-drawn map. The county was divided into ranches, heavy black lines marking the boundaries, while Colson and other towns were inked in with a lighter hand and set apart with a lopsided star.

The door clicked shut and Jackson halted beside her, his gaze following hers to the map.

"I think old Eli's grandfather drew that," he commented. "He was a surveyor for the U.S. government before he came west and homesteaded this place."

"Fascinating," Rebecca murmured. "He would have been your great-great-grandfather?"

"Something like that." Jackson shrugged. "Eli was my great-uncle, but I'm not sure exactly how the family tree shakes out."

"Did you grow up here?" Her gaze found his name printed in neat black ink beneath the faded letters spelling out "Eli Kuhlman." The expanse of land that surrounded the names appeared enormous.

"Hell, no," Jackson said shortly. "I never knew about Eli or this ranch until I got a letter from an attorney telling me that he'd died and left it to me."

"Oh." She wanted to ask him why he hadn't known that he had a great-uncle who owned an enormous property. She glanced sideways at him. His attention was focused on the big map, his eyes narrowed, the lines of his face taut and forbidding.

Despite her curiosity, caution kept her from questioning him further.

His gaze left the map and met hers for a brief second before he looked away.

"The computer is new," he said abruptly, gesturing toward the desk where several unopened boxes were stacked on the floor, the top one even with the desktop. "I haven't unpacked it yet."

He walked to the desk and Rebecca followed, noting that the brand name stamped on the boxes was a computer she particularly favored. Jackson pulled out the old-fashioned desk chair, the oiled casters rolling quietly over the scarred wooden floor.

"Have a seat."

It was more an order than a polite invitation but Rebecca didn't comment. Instead, she seated herself in the worn, brown leather chair while Jackson snagged a straight-backed oaken chair and dragged it nearer the desk. His scent surrounded her, an indefinable mix of soap and male. Awareness shivered up her spine, lifting the fine hairs at her nape.

"These are the ledgers for the last thirty years." Jackson reached across the desk and picked up a stack of books, setting them squarely on the bare oak desktop in front of Rebecca. The hardcover green ledgers, worn from use and faded with age, had entries in a spidery, often illegible hand.

For the next hour, Jackson explained the handwritten bookkeeping system that the previous owner, Eli

Kuhlman, had used. Reading the notes soon had Rebecca's eyes aching from strain.

The greatest strain, however, came from being in such close proximity to Jackson. He straddled the chair, his forearms crossed along the square wooden back. On one occasion, he stood and leaned over her at the desk, pointing out and explaining an item in a ledger, his arm twice brushing against hers. Waiting for him to touch her again had her nerves strung taut until she wanted to scream with tension.

By the time Jackson left to make a last check of the barns and she climbed the stairs to bed, her nerves were jangling.

Chapter Two

Jackson stacked his hands beneath his head and stared up at the ceiling. Outside the bedroom window, one of the maples' far-reaching branches scratched gently against the glass pane. The three-quarter moon threw leaf-shaped shadows across the white ceiling, the dark shapes shifting and changing with the faint breeze.

He still didn't know what he was going to do about Rebecca Wallingford.

She represented a complication that he didn't have time to deal with. He was up to his neck in work, putting in fourteen-hour days to finish upgrading the ranch's buildings and fences. He hadn't been too wild about the idea of having a representative of the investment company underfoot, but the unexpected offer of financing from the San Francisco firm had arrived after he'd been turned down by every bank within a five-hundred-mile radius of Colson. Eli Kuhlman had left him land worth millions but no cash assets, and the fences, buildings and machinery were all desperately in need of repair. He'd reached the point where he would have done anything short of a criminal act to get the money to develop the ranch. When he was told that the accountant would be a fifty-three-year-old man named Walter Andersen, he'd resigned himself to squeezing one more boarder into the house for a few months. He'd hoped that Walter could at least play a decent game of poker.

Then Rebecca arrived. One look at her green eyes and curvy body had his temperature rising.

"Hell," he muttered. Two or three long months. Maybe it was a good thing he had enough work to keep him busy twenty-four hours a day, if needed. Because there was no way he was acting on his instinct to ignore the engagement ring on her finger and pursue her. He had a hard-and-fast rule—never date anyone you work with—and he never broke it. Never. He'd been down that road and lived to regret it. He wasn't going there again.

Rebecca had difficulty falling asleep. Accustomed as she was to the sounds of traffic and the occasional siren from the street below her sixth-story apartment windows in downtown San Francisco, the complete silence surrounding the ranch house was unsettling. But if it was strangely quiet outside, inside, Rebecca's thoughts were uncharacteristically chaotic.

What was she going to do about the impact Jackson Rand had on her senses? Despite her earlier confidence that she could control her body's reaction to the rancher, she hadn't been able to shut down her response to him in the office. Would she become more adept at ignoring him with time? Or less so?

Thank goodness I never have to worry about any of this with Steven, she thought. Life with Steven would be comfortable and placid, with no disturbing wakes and whitecaps, no turbulent waters to threaten the calm comfort of their life together.

She woke the next morning to the sound of water running in the bathroom next door and the muted sounds of men's voices, followed by the thud of boots on stair treads. Disoriented, she lay still, staring at the ceiling for a moment before she remembered where she was.

She turned her head and squinted at her small alarm clock on the night table.

Five o'clock? Her body was still on San Francisco Pacific time, where it was only 3:00 a.m. She groaned aloud and rolled over, pulling the sheet and blanket over her head.

The maneuver didn't help. Fifteen minutes later,

she shoved the covers back and glared at the clock. The luminous dial glowed silently back at her.

It's no use. She admitted finally and tossed back the covers. Groping for her ankle-length robe at the end of the bed, she pulled it on over her pajamas, shoved her feet into matching white terry-cloth mules and took her toiletry bag from the top of the dresser. If she couldn't sleep, she thought, she may as well get up, get dressed and get to work.

The hall was silent when she stepped out of her bedroom. In the vacant bathroom, damp towels hung over the racks, droplets of water dotted the sink and the faint scent of mint toothpaste hung in the warm air.

She splashed her face, brushed her teeth, ran a brush through her hair and caught it up into a high ponytail, then left the bathroom.

She moved quietly down the stairs, drawn by the irresistible smell of brewed coffee, and paused to listen intently at the bottom of the steps. The house was quiet. Breathing a sigh of relief that she had the house to herself, she walked down the hall and was two steps into the kitchen before she halted abruptly. Jackson was seated at the table, a coffee mug cradled in his hand.

"Good morning," she managed, her voice husky with sleep.

"Good morning."

His deep drawl curled her toes inside her slippers

and made her feel much too vulnerable in her half-awake state.

Caffeine. I need caffeine.

She crossed the room to the counter, took down a mug and filled it, grimacing at the first strong, black sip.

"Something wrong with the coffee?"

She looked up. Jackson's eyes held amusement.

"Not at all. It's just that I usually drink tea in the morning and coffee later. Tea isn't quite as strong as coffee."

"The only kind of tea I ever drink is iced and loaded with sugar," he commented.

Rebecca wondered if all Montana men felt this way about tea, since this was exactly what Hank had told her yesterday.

The growl of powerful truck engines sounded outside.

"The lumber delivery must be here." He stood and pulled out a chair. "Have a seat."

He walked toward the counter, passing Rebecca as she headed for the table.

"Make yourself at home. If you need anything today or have any questions about the books, I'll be down at the barn. Or if it can wait, we usually break for lunch around noon."

He filled a thermal mug with coffee, snapped the lid on and headed for the back door, pausing to look down at her as he passed the table. "You all right?"

"What? Oh, yes." She yawned. "Really. I'm just not awake yet." She added when he looked unconvinced.

"If you say so." He shot her one last look and left the kitchen, the screen door slapping softly shut behind him.

Rebecca groaned and dropped her face into her hands.

I can barely think early in the morning, let alone deal with him.

All that sex appeal should come with a warning label, she thought, getting up to put the kettle on. Coffee just wasn't a substitute for a strong cup of tea first thing in the morning.

Revived by hot tea and toast, Rebecca headed back up the stairs to shower and dress for the day in a lightweight white skirt, matching top and sandals. By seven o'clock, she was opening the office door, laptop and briefcase in hand.

Much to her surprise, she found the computer unpacked, the heavy monitor, CPU and keyboard sitting on the desktop, while the printer stood on a table placed at a right angle on the far side of the desk.

"Jackson must have unpacked it last night after I went to bed," she mused.

Touched by his consideration, she took time to plug in her laptop to check her e-mail, then pulled out her cell phone. The phone didn't respond with a dial tone, however, and she switched to the desktop phone. It took only a few moments to check her phone messages at her apartment, but much longer when she connected to her office voice mail. Her pen flew across the paper as she jotted down names, phone numbers and noted priorities, making a mental note to check her electronic daytimer before e-mailing her secretary with instructions.

Satisfied that her responsibilities in San Francisco were taken care of, she connected the cables and plugged in Jackson's new desktop computer. Green, red and amber lights blinked and the CPU hummed with a satisfactory, familiar sound. She installed her favorite software and loaded the programs Jackson had bought to address specific ranching issues, including a spreadsheet to track the breeding program. She found the programs surprisingly fascinating.

At ten o'clock, she glanced at her watch and reached for the phone. It was eight o'clock in San Francisco and her mother's secretary promptly put her through to Kathleen.

"Hi, Mom."

"Good morning, Rebecca. How was your flight?"

"Fine, except for the truly terrible lunch the airline served in first class. I had rubber chicken again."

Kathleen's chuckle warmed the phone line. Rebecca eased back in the swivel wooden desk chair and stretched out her legs, propping her feet on the round metal wastebasket beneath the desk.

"Other than that, how are things going? Are you settled in?"

"Sort of."

"What do you mean 'sort of'? Weren't your rooms ready?"

"Not rooms. Room, Mom, singular. One bedroom, which is fine. The bed is comfortable and that's the most important thing. The problem is that the house has four bedrooms, one of which is mine. The other three are occupied by the four men who work here on the ranch. And Mr. Rand seems to think that the two youngest ones will fight over dating me while the third man, Hank, who I'm guessing is somewhere in his seventies, hates women and wants me to leave."

"What about Jackson Rand?" Kathleen asked after a short silence.

Rebecca had a quick mental image of Jackson's abrupt departure earlier that morning. "I suspect that he strongly wishes that I would leave, too, but he's stuck with me and he knows it."

Kathleen's sigh was clearly audible over the line separating Montana and San Francisco. "Good grief. Why can't these things ever be simple?"

Rebecca laughed. She was familiar with her mother's long struggle to survive in a male-dominated business world. "Because of the never ending battle of the sexes." She quoted her mother's oft heard comment. "It's going to be fine, Mom."

"Are you sure you're safe living in the house with these men?"

Kathleen's concern was clear and Rebecca hastened to reassure her. "Absolutely, Mom. I'm not the slightest bit worried about safety. It's just going to take a while to convince Mr. Rand that I'm not going to encourage either of the younger members of his crew, and that I can win over Hank. By the way," she added, grinning, "Hank reminds me of Mr. Althorpe."

"Hmm. Maybe you can bribe him with chocolate."

"Exactly what I wondered."

The two women shared a companionable, understanding moment of silence.

"So," Kathleen said briskly. "What can you tell me about the business?"

Rebecca told her what little she'd learned about Jackson's operation in a brief, concise report. "I haven't had a tour of the facility yet, but plan to ask Mr. Rand to show me around tonight after work. Mom," she paused, wondering how to word her question and opting for bluntness. "I have to confess, I'm baffled as to why you want me to stay here for so long. The operation seems fairly straightforward. I understand that you want to keep a close eye on Bay Area's money since this is our first investment in this type of business, but I could just as easily have flown in for a few days and then come back in a month or two to check on the status of the business. I'm not sure what it is you expect me to do every day that will keep me busy for a few months."

Kathleen's hesitation was so brief that if Rebecca didn't know her so intimately, she might have missed it.

"I'd rather err on the side of caution, Rebecca. With you on-site, I know we'll have instant input if there are any problems with Mr. Rand's business plans going forward. And besides," she added, "you haven't had a vacation in four years. It's about time you drew an assignment with enough downtime to let you relax."

"I'm not sure that I need a vacation," Rebecca replied, unconvinced that Kathleen was telling her all of her reasons, but knowing that her mother wouldn't share the whole story until she was ready. "But if you want me here, I'm sure I'll find plenty to occupy my time."

"Good," Kathleen replied. "I'd like you to check in with the attorney, Victoria Bowdrie, in Colson today. She has some documents that need to be signed and, instead of having them forwarded here to the central office, I've authorized you to sign on behalf of the company."

"All right. I'll drive in this morning, it'll give me an opportunity to get my bearings and check out the shopping in Colson."

Kathleen laughed. "That's my girl."

"Bye, Mom."

Kathleen rang off and Rebecca tidied up the desk, shut down the computer and headed upstairs to collect her purse and car keys.

Jackson was in the hayloft of the big barn, tearing out broken floorboards and replacing them with new planks. The huge doors stood open at each end of the loft, the slight cross-breeze doing little to cool the midmorning heat trapped beneath the rafters. He hammered a nail home and stood, wiping his brow with the back of his forearm as he walked to the open door where it was several degrees cooler. He picked up a five-gallon thermos jug off the floor just inside the door and held it aloft, twisting the spout to let the water pour over his head and shoulders before lowering it to his mouth. The cool water felt as good going down his throat as it had cascading over his torso, the slight breeze cooling him further as it flowed over his wet chest and arms.

The day promised to be another scorcher, he reflected, wondering just how hot it was.

The slap of wood against wood sounded clearly across the ranch yard. Jackson glanced toward the house and went still, the water jug forgotten in his hand.

Rebecca descended the porch steps, legs and arms tan against a white skirt and short-sleeved top. Her hair was loose, brushing against her throat and the boat-neck white top. She carried a small purse and a slim black leather briefcase.

Jackson leaned one shoulder against the door frame and watched as she walked down the path to the fence, opened and closed the gate, then rounded the front of her car and slid beneath the wheel.

What the hell am I going to do about her? He shook his head as she drove away, aware of the tighter fit of his jeans. *Just watching her walk turns me on.* Irritated, he turned back to the waiting broken floorboards.

Unaware she'd been observed, Rebecca retraced her journey from yesterday, but this time, she wasn't as travel-weary and was able to take in more details of her surroundings. The land stretching away from each side of the road was as different from San Francisco as the earth from Mars. Instead of urban streets and glimpses of the sparkling blue waters of the Bay from the city's steep, crowded hills, Rebecca saw a patchwork of green wheat fields and the black dirt of plowed land. The cultivated fields were interspersed with rough pastures dotted with silvery sagebrush. Large, often flat-topped buttes rose to loom over fields and pastures and above it all, the dome of endless, bright blue sky stretched without a cloud in sight.

As much as she appreciated San Francisco's charm, Rebecca felt drawn to this extremely different landscape with a deep pull on her emotions that felt oddly as if she had come home.

Which was silly, she reflected. She'd never before visited Montana, let alone called this area home.

Dismissing the notion, Rebecca switched off the air conditioner, rolled down the window and luxuriated in the clean, sage-scented air that blew in, tangling her hair and sending it skeining across her face, her sunglasses keeping the strands out of her eyes.

The bright sunlight, already hot though it was only June, heated her bare arm. Rebecca wasn't used to real summer heat. In San Francisco, the breeze off the Pacific cooled even the hottest days.

And I'll be here for a few months, she reflected. *Which means that perhaps I'll see the fall season, too.* The thought was appealing. Raised in the mild climate of California's Pacific Coast, she hadn't experienced the changing of seasons with the same degree of intensity Montana residents were accustomed to seeing.

The weather is one of those unique-to-the-area things that I told Jackson I'd find to enjoy here. She felt smug satisfaction that barely a day after he'd doubted that she'd find anything of interest in Colson, she had already proved him wrong.

Strange not to be stuck in traffic, nor to smell exhaust and be hit by noise with the car window down, she thought idly.

She crested a hill and below her lay the small

ranching community of Colson. Slowing at the out-
skirts, she checked her directions. Deciding that the
attorney's Main Street address was most likely in the
center of town, she turned right at the next cross
street. A large, flat-roofed building on one corner had
a big neon sign declaring that the Crossroads Bar and
Grill was open for business. She wondered briefly if
the Crossroads was the local version of a singles' bar.

Rebecca drove through a residential area with old
Victorian houses set back amid immaculate green
lawns and beds of roses, peonies, marigolds and alys-
sum that bloomed profusely; majestic old maples
shaded the wide streets. Without a map, she relied on
instinct, turning left. Houses gradually gave way to
commercial buildings, and in moments Rebecca
found Main Street.

"Dennings Pharmacy, Annie's Cafe," she murmured aloud, noting that the street numbers were
climbing higher. *At least I'm going in the right direction.*

The attorney's office was tucked between the First
National Bank and Marnie's Dress Shop, the gold let-
tering on the spotless window reading "Foslund and
Bowdrie, Attorneys at Law."

Rebecca angled the car into the curb and switched
off the engine, gathering her purse and briefcase.

A bell jangled as she opened the office door, and
the pleasant-faced woman behind the reception desk
looked up, smiling a welcome.

"Good morning. Can I help you?"

"Yes. I don't have an appointment but I wonder if Victoria Bowdrie is available?"

"I'll check. May I tell her who's calling?"

"Rebecca Wallingford of Bay Area Investments."

Moments later, a petite blonde in a cream summer business suit followed the secretary into the outer office where Rebecca stood.

"Ms. Wallingford? I'm Victoria Bowdrie." Smiling, she held out her hand.

"It's a pleasure to meet you, and please call me Rebecca." She returned the smile and shook the attorney's hand. "I spoke with my mother this morning and she asked me to see you today. I believe you have some documents that need to be signed?"

"Ah, yes, of course." Victoria waved Rebecca ahead of her and into the inner office. "An addendum to the original contract that addresses your review reports and release-of-funds dates. Have a seat, Rebecca."

Rebecca dropped into one of two leather chairs facing the polished oak desk while Victoria took a seat behind the desk and collected a folder from a wooden tray. She opened it and handed her a sheaf of papers across the glossy desktop. "I think you'll find these self-explanatory."

Silence reigned while Rebecca carefully read the pages of legal jargon, puzzlement growing before she finished and looked up at Victoria.

''I'm sorry, but I'm afraid I don't see any outstanding differences between this document and the original in my file.''

Victoria chuckled. ''The changes are fairly small, but your mother wanted the details clarified.'' She flipped a page on her copy of the document, scanning quickly until she found what she was looking for. ''If you'll look at page two, paragraph four, I believe you'll find that the due date on your first report is moved back two days, with the resulting release of funds to Mr. Rand upon receipt of a favorable review by Bay Area Corporate Office to be moved back an equal amount of time.''

Rebecca reread the paragraph, noted the dates and pulled her electronic daytimer from her leather briefcase. Victoria was right, she thought, the dates were changed by two days in each instance.

Odd that Kathleen wanted her to sign the revised documents immediately, she thought with a frown. But then, she mentally shrugged, it gave her a good excuse to visit Colson and see what the town was like.

Ten minutes later, Rebecca stepped out of the office, pulled the door closed behind her, and glanced up and down the wide main street. She took a few moments to return her briefcase to her car and then strolled down the sidewalk to window-shop. Murphy's Market yielded her favorite brand of English Breakfast tea and browsing the aisles of Dennings

Pharmacy added a new bottle of hot-pink nail polish to her bag.

Rebecca strolled down one side of Main Street and halfway up the other when she reached Annie's Cafe. An elderly gentleman pushed open the door and stepped briskly out to move off down the sidewalk. The aromas that wafted out to Rebecca through the briefly open door reminded her that it was nearly lunchtime and that more than a few hours had passed since she'd eaten a piece of toast for breakfast.

Forty minutes later, replete with homemade soup and a delicious turkey sandwich on wheat that was the luncheon special, Rebecca left the cafe, pausing to hold the door open for a group of older women entering.

The first two ladies smiled absentmindedly and murmured, "Thank you," but the third glanced at Rebecca and halted abruptly, her eyes widening in shock, her face visibly paling.

"Who are you?" the older woman demanded.

Taken aback, Rebecca stared at the woman for a second before finding her voice. "I beg your pardon?"

"Who are you?" the woman demanded again. "And what are you doing in Colson?"

"I'm not sure that's any of your business." Rebecca eyed the woman. "Do I know you, ma'am?"

"You most certainly do not. Nor are you likely to." The woman drew herself up, chin lifting haughtily. "And let me warn you, miss, whatever you're planning, it won't work."

"I have no idea what you're talking about." Rebecca was beginning to wonder if the woman had mistaken her for someone else.

"Don't play the innocent with me," the woman said. "Just because you've got Charlie's green eyes and black hair doesn't prove a thing."

"You must have me confused with someone else."

"And if you stir up that old scandal again, you'll be sorry," the woman went on, as if Rebecca hadn't spoken.

This time, she didn't answer. Instead, she pointedly took a step back and held the door wider.

The impeccably dressed woman tilted her chin higher and swept past Rebecca and into the cafe.

Shaking her head in puzzlement, Rebecca paused on the curb, waiting for a truck to pass before crossing the wide street to her car. The drive back to the Rand Ranch gave her plenty of time to go over the strange conversation, but when she drove into the ranch yard and braked in front of the house, Jackson pushed open the screen door and the sight of him drove the incident from her mind.

Annoyed at the swift surge of pleasure that quickened her heartbeat and breathing, she drew a deep breath, gathered her briefcase, purse and light shopping bag and left the car.

She joined him on the porch, aware that his gaze

hadn't left her on the walk from car to house. "Hello," she said pleasantly, proud of hard-won composure that kept her voice even.

"Afternoon." He held the door for her. "If you don't have something you need to do right now, I thought I'd take you on a tour of the outbuildings. Or we can do it after dinner tonight, if you'd rather."

"No, now is fine." Business, she reminded herself. This is business and he's just another client. "Give me ten minutes to change into jeans and I'll be right with you."

Jackson nodded. Rebecca hurried up the stairs, dropped her packages on the bed and pulled jeans and a cotton shirt from their hangers. She stripped off the white skirt and top, quickly slipped them onto the two hangers she'd just emptied, and stepped into the jeans, yanking them up her legs and shrugging into the pale blue shirt. She buttoned the shirt with swift efficiency and tucked it into the waistband of her jeans before slipping a belt into the jean loops.

It took only moments to locate a pair of socks in her drawer, pull them on and tug on worn but polished brown hiking boots, lacing them with quick movements. Although she'd never hiked in the California mountains, she loved the boots for their practical toughness in the city's winter rain and cold.

She glanced in the mirror, smoothed her hair with a few quick strokes of her brush and left the room.

Jackson was standing just where she'd left him, his

hat tugged low over his brow, arms crossed, one shoulder leaning against the porch post, staring out across the rolling pasture that stretched to the buttes edging the horizon.

He turned when Rebecca pushed the screen door open, his gaze sweeping her from head to toe in one swift glance, generating a surge of heat.

"You should wear a hat," he commented, plucking a straw cowboy hat from the seat of a rocking chair and handing it to her. "The sun can be dangerous if you're not used to it."

"Thanks." Rebecca ignored the rush of awareness when his fingers brushed hers. His long strides made nearly two of hers, and he was ahead of her before they reached the gate. He glanced back at her and immediately slowed.

"Sorry." He held the gate wide and Rebecca went through ahead of him. "The basic structure of most of the buildings was solid, but all of them needed a lot of work." They set off across the lot toward the outbuildings. "A couple of cattle sheds were too far gone to save so we pulled them down. We'll rebuild them after finishing the repairs to the barn."

"What happened? Why did the previous owner allow the buildings to deteriorate so badly?" Rebecca asked as they stepped from the hot sunlight into the shadowy barn. Curious, she gazed upward, her eye drawn to the aged rafters visible through a hole in the hayloft floor above her. The pungent scent of raw lumber mingled with the lingering smells of hay, leather and animals.

"I doubt he meant to," Jackson answered. "But he was over ninety years old when he passed on, and from what the neighbors tell me, he was a recluse. Running this ranch alone would be a tough job for a young man, let alone a man as old as Eli. Not only are there buildings and equipment to maintain, but miles of fence to repair. At the end, he was running only a few head of cattle and most of those were wild as jackrabbits. I doubt he even knew how many he had."

"Do you?"

"Do I what?" He glanced at her, a small frown drawing a *V* between his eyebrows.

"Do you know how many cattle you have?"

He shook his head. "I haven't got a clue. I haven't had time to ride the pastures and round up the cattle that belonged to old Eli. I spend most Saturdays or Sundays riding the fence line, trying to keep enough strands of wire upright to hold the few wild steers and cows that belong to me on Rand pasture and off of Bowdrie grass."

"Bowdrie? Is that Victoria Bowdrie? Is she your neighbor?" Rebecca asked with interest.

"Cully and Quinn Bowdrie own the spread to the west of me and Victoria is Quinn's wife. Why?"

"No reason. I met Victoria Bowdrie today, in fact. She's the reason I went into Colson this morning.

There were a couple of small changes to your contract that I had to initial.''

"The wording that moved the due dates of your reports and the payment delivery dates?" he asked.

"Yes."

"You folks are always so picky about a couple of days?" he asked, eyeing her with curiosity.

"We at Bay Area Investments prefer to call it 'paying attention to detail,'" she responded with a touch of wry humor. Her stepfather had been a stickler for small details and her mother continued the practice. Still, she wondered why her mother had insisted that she personally initial the minor changes to the contract. She also wondered why her mother had wanted it done immediately.

The list of things that baffled Rebecca about her mother's directions for handling the Rand Ranch investment was growing longer by the day.

Chapter Three

"I suppose keeping all the details clear makes your job easier," Jackson commented.

"Yes," she responded. "It does." She glanced away from him and up at the ceiling again. "What happened there?" She pointed at the hole in the hayloft floor.

"The roof directly above leaked and the moisture rotted the planks. We've repaired the roof, but haven't had time to replace the flooring yet. Several sections of the barn still need work." He curved his hand around a support post, muscles flexing as he tested its stability. "But the majority of the structure is solid. The bull barn is through here."

Rebecca followed him down the center aisle of the old barn. A door stood open at the far end and she stepped through into a smaller building that was clearly a new addition. Here, the individual box stalls were roomy with high, sturdy walls. Curious, she silently counted the number of thick gates standing open down the wide alley.

"How many bulls do you plan to keep here?"

"I'll have space for a dozen in this building, but at the moment, I only have one." He led the way to a stall at the far end. "This is Tiny."

Rebecca peered through the narrow opening between two of the heavy planks. "Tiny?" She glanced at Jackson in disbelief. His swift smile sent a jolt of electricity shivering up her spine.

"His registered name is too long to pronounce, so Hank gave him a nickname."

"And he picked Tiny?" Rebecca stared at the massive animal. She'd never been this close to a purebred bull before, but he seemed huge, his reddish-brown coat marked with white at his head, lower legs and the tip of his tail. He stood placidly, eyeing her calmly.

"Hank has a quirky sense of humor."

Rebecca glanced quickly at Jackson but he was looking at the bull and she couldn't tell if he was joking. "I see."

"Tiny is the first." Jackson gestured at the empty stalls on each side. "Within six months, I want to have this barn full.'' He turned, waiting for Rebecca to fall in step with him before walking outside. New posts and wire fencing marched in a gleaming straight line away from the building. ''We fenced this pasture for Tiny. After we finish upgrading the buildings, we'll start fencing the rest of the pasture land to hold heifers. I'll breed them to the bulls and sell the calves, which will allow the ranch to maximize use of all the acreage and the availability of our own bulls.''

''It sounds like a huge project,'' Rebecca commented.

''It is,'' Jackson agreed. ''A lot of work and a big initial investment, but well worth it in the long run.''

Rebecca shaded her eyes against the hot sun, her gaze sweeping over the fenced area where they stood and a corral on the far side of the barn. A muscular bay quarter horse inside the enclosure lifted his head and pricked his ears, nickering softly. ''You have horses?''

''Of course.''

''How many?''

''Six.''

They walked toward the corral and Rebecca felt his sidelong glance as surely as if he'd touched her. But she was determined not to react.

''What do you use them for?''

''Rounding up cattle, riding fence lines, just about anything we can that doesn't require a truck. I'd rather ride a horse than drive a pickup.'' They reached the corral fence and stopped. The bay horse stretched his head toward them over the top rail, and Jackson rubbed his forehead between his well-shaped ears, pushing the black forelock aside. "This is Shorty."

"Shorty?" Rebecca laughed. The bay was tall for a quarter horse, his legs long. "Let me guess, Hank named him?"

"Yeah, as a matter of fact he did. How did you know?"

"Just a wild guess."

The sound of an engine disturbed the quiet afternoon. A truck sped toward them on the gravel ranch road that led to the highway, a cloud of dust billowing in its wake.

"That must be Mick." Jackson glanced at his watch. "I have to get back to work on the barn. You've seen most of the current construction, but if there's anything else you think you need to see, we can come back after dinner."

"I've seen enough to send my home office a preliminary report. Perhaps you can give me a tour of the remaining outbuildings later this week?"

"Sure." Jackson pointed at several outbuildings on the far side of the barn. "We haven't done any work on them yet, but the granaries and machine shop are in better shape than the barn."

"That's fortunate." Rebecca stroked her palm down Shorty's nose before turning away.

They crossed a short expanse of grass to the gate

set into the fence where it met the corner of the barn. Jackson unlatched the heavy gate, the powerful muscles in his shoulders, biceps and forearms flexing as he pulled it open. Her arm accidentally brushed his as she walked past him and through the opening, and the air crackled with swift electricity. Startled, she glanced up. Her gaze collided with Jackson's and found the same hot awareness that slammed into her, stealing her breath. She faltered before tearing her gaze from his and stepping quickly away from the fence. She was several strides ahead of him by the time he refastened the gate and followed.

"Thanks for the tour." He was still a step behind her when she spoke.

"No problem."

She lifted a hand in response to Mick's greeting but kept walking, determined to remove herself from temptation, angling toward the house while Jackson strode toward the truck parked in front of the barn.

She climbed the steps and let herself into the house, closing the screen door quietly behind her and shutting Jackson out of sight.

That man's lethal. He practically oozes testosterone. Deciding that it would be wise if she avoided spending time alone with Jackson in future, she headed for the office to make notes on the progress of repair and new construction she'd seen on her short tour. The report she later e-mailed to her mother was concise and analytical, reflecting none of her concern over the electricity that arced between her and Jackson.

Rebecca's second day on the Rand Ranch started like the first—much too early. This time, it was the clatter of boots on the stairs that woke her. She opened one eye and looked at her alarm clock. The hands pointed to 5:00 a.m., and she groaned aloud before she rolled over and looked out the window. Although sunlight wasn't pouring through the pane, the gray dawn outside was quickly lightening and would soon give way to the rising sun.

She turned onto her back and stared at the ceiling, listening to the muted sounds of voices drifting up the stairway. Then the distinctive sound of the door to the utility porch opening and closing reached her ears, followed by the sound of the outside door doing the same.

Quiet reigned in the house once again, but unfortunately for Rebecca, she was wide awake. She sat up, stretched her hands toward the ceiling, yawning, then tossed back the blankets and rose, sliding her feet into slippers and her arms into her robe. She pulled open the door and paused to listen, but heard no deep rumble of masculine voices so she hurried into the bathroom. When she entered the kitchen moments later, the room was empty, and only four coffee mugs, rinsed and turned upside down on the drying rack at the sink, testified that Jackson and his crew had recently eaten breakfast. Rebecca ran fresh water into the teakettle and switched on the stove's burner before taking out tea bags and a heavy white crockery mug.

An hour later, showered and dressed for the day, she stirred sugar into her second mug of tea and wandered outside on the porch. The sun was a hot golden globe in a brilliant blue sky, but in the shade of the porch where the sun's rays couldn't reach, the morning air was still cool. Rebecca dropped into one of the worn oak rockers, drawing her light jacket closer around her shoulders as she sipped her tea. The rolling pastures of the ranch gradually rose to meet the bulk of a towering butte against the horizon, and she wondered how many miles lay between it and the ranch buildings. Several horses grazed in a smaller fenced pasture near the buildings, their glossy hides gleaming beneath the early morning sun.

The novelty of sitting idly on a porch with her morning mug of tea was so unusual that Rebecca couldn't help but smile. Unstructured time, with no urgency to begin a daily list of "to do" items, was both liberating and oddly disconcerting. All in all, she decided, there was something to be said for freedom from her normal fast-paced routine and fighting the city's rush-hour traffic.

Maybe Mom was right. Maybe I do need a vacation.

She still wasn't convinced, but she was willing to make the most of her lighter workload.

She returned her mug to the kitchen and packed a thermos of water, a sandwich and an apple into her small knapsack and took a carrot from the refrigerator bin. Then she collected the straw hat Jackson had loaned her the day before and went in search of the rancher. She found him in the barn.

He was on a ladder, hammering nails into new lumber to patch a section of wall. The old boards had been removed, leaving a hole to the outside. Fortunately for Rebecca's vow to remain unaffected by him, the interior of the barn was still cool, and he hadn't stripped off his shirt.

"Jackson?"

He didn't respond. Deciding that he probably couldn't hear her over the sound of his hammering and the whine of the saw from another room, Rebecca tried again, a little louder. "Jackson."

He stopped hammering and looked over his shoulder at her.

"I wonder if I could borrow one of the horses? I thought I'd go riding early before it gets too hot."

His gaze swept her from head to toe, clearly skeptical. "You can ride?"

"Yes."

He descended the ladder, hooking the hammer over one of the rungs. "How well?"

"I do okay." He continued to stare at her, obviously waiting for her to elaborate. "I've ridden since I was a little girl. My mother and I board horses at a stable in a town across the Golden Gate Bridge."

"What kind of horses?" His voice was curious.

"Thoroughbreds."

He raised an eyebrow but didn't comment. "I've got a nice little mare that might be good. She has an easy gait."

Rebecca swallowed a hasty retort. She didn't think he'd be convinced of her riding ability by anything she said. She suspected that Jackson would need to see for himself that she could be trusted with his mare.

"She sounds perfect."

It didn't take Jackson long to catch the mare and saddle her. Rebecca held the bridle, stroking the white blaze that started between the mare's wide-set, intelligent eyes and curved over her nostrils and below her chin. She took the carrot from her jeans pocket, snapped off a chunk and held it on the flat of her palm. The mare's soft lips tickled her palm as she took the treat, and Rebecca laughed, glancing up to see Jackson watching her.

"She likes carrots," she said, suddenly nervous under his unreadable gaze.

"She likes sugar lumps, too. Also apples. Pretty much anything you have in your pocket, she'll eat. She's a cheap date."

Rebecca laughed and gave the horse the last of the carrot. "What's her name?"

"Sadie." He took her knapsack of food from atop a nearby grain bag and tucked it into the saddlebag, then tugged the reins out of her hands. "If you're going to ride before the day heats up, you'd better get going."

She walked beside him, leaving the shade of the barn for the bright sunlight. He halted and Rebecca swung into the saddle.

"How are the stirrups?"

"A little long, I think."

"Stand up."

Rebecca stood, waiting until he ran an expert glance over her before he nodded. When she sat down, Jackson's hand closed over the back of her calf and tugged her foot out of the stirrup.

Although he quickly released her, Rebecca's muscle tingled from the warmth and strength of his hand. He was far too close as he adjusted the stirrup, the brim of his straw hat nearly brushing against her jeans-covered thigh.

"Try it now."

He tilted his head, looking up at her, and Rebecca was stunned by the impact when his gaze found hers. For a moment, they seemed caught in the web of electricity that spun between them. Then she wrenched her gaze from his and slipped her boot into the stirrup.

''That's much better.'' Despite her best efforts, her voice was throatier than normal.

''Good.'' He tested the strap before ducking beneath the mare's neck.

Rebecca pulled her foot from the left stirrup and Jackson unbuckled, adjusted and rebuckled the strap with swift ease, giving it a sharp tug to test it before lowering the stirrup.

''Thank you.''

''No problem.'' He caught the bridle and held the mare. ''Stay in the home pasture and you can't get lost. If you lose sight of the ranch buildings, just ride due east and sooner or later, you'll reach a fence line. Follow the fence line and eventually you'll find yourself back at the ranch.''

''All right.''

''And don't stay out too long. The temperature is likely to climb over ninety today and you aren't used to the heat. If you're not back by noon, one of us will have to come looking for you.''

He didn't add that he would be extremely annoyed if he or any of his crew had to search for her, but Rebecca was sure that he would be. ''I'll be back before noon.''

''Good.'' He pointed to a gate in the fence at the far western corner of the barn. ''I'll open the gate for you.''

Rebecca could feel his gaze as she lifted the reins and walked the mare toward the fence. She knew that she would do the same if an unfamiliar rider were up on her horse in California. Still, some part of her was annoyed that he was judging her riding ability.

She walked Sadie through the open gate, nodded at Jackson and lifted the little mare into a trot. Her irritation with Jackson was quickly forgotten in the delight of riding once again. Sadie was even-tempered and surefooted, and Rebecca gave herself over to the pleasure of riding across the rolling acres. At first she followed a well-defined, narrow track along the fence line, then a small grove of trees lured her to explore. She found a natural spring on the edge of the dozen or so trees and a stainless-steel watering tank with water spilling over its side, surrounded by cattle hoofprints, sunk deep into the soft, wet ground. No cows were present, however, so she let the mare drink and then followed another well-used track around the curve of a small hill.

Despite the fact that she was thousands of miles from San Francisco, something about the land reminded her of the California hills she normally rode. The dry air was pungent with the scent of sagebrush growing in gray-green clumps and the rolling hills were punctuated by dry arroyos.

Although they probably weren't called arroyos, she reflected as Sadie picked her way down the side of a wash, her hooves sliding on small rocks before gaining traction. Rebecca wondered what the Montana equivalent was for the Spanish word.

She returned to the ranch just before eleven-thirty, sighing with relief as she left the burning heat of the sun behind and rode into the barn's cool interior. The building was oddly quiet, with no sounds of hammer, saw or the deep timbre of masculine voices.

In the kitchen, Hank, Mitch and Gib were making thick ham sandwiches for lunch. Jackson glanced at his watch, frowned and left them teasing Gib about the amount of food on his plate while he walked to the front hall and looked out the screen door. He reached the doorway just in time to see Rebecca and the mare disappear into the dim interior of the barn.

Relief that she was home safe washed over him, followed swiftly by denial. He would have been worried about anyone not used to the heat and a stranger to the land; there wasn't anything unusual about his concern for her.

His first instinct was to walk to the barn and unsaddle the mare. His second was to stay where he was and let her take care of the mare herself. His first instinct won.

"How was your ride?"

Concentrating on loosening the saddle girth, Rebecca was startled by Jackson's deep voice. She looked over her shoulder to see him striding toward her and she straightened. "Wonderful."

His gaze flicked over her face before his hands closed over her biceps. He shifted her aside and took her place, quickly and efficiently unbuckling the girth and sliding the blanket and saddle off the horse. "You didn't have any trouble finding your way home?"

"No." Rebecca didn't have time to protest that she could take care of the mare before he settled the saddle over a sawhorse and returned with a clean feed sack to begin rubbing down the mare. She picked up a brush and started grooming Sadie's sweat-damp hide with brisk strokes. "You were right about the heat," she commented, bending to sweep the brush over the mare's belly where the girth had left a dark band.

He paused, his gaze narrowing. "Did you drink water while you were out? Are you feeling dizzy?"

"I feel fine and I drank lots of water. In fact, I emptied the water bottle I carried with me and stopped at the stock tank to refill it on my way home."

"You didn't drink out of the tank, did you?"

Rebecca laughed. "No. I took it from the pipe connected to the pump."

"Good."

The relief on his face made her smile. "Did you think I was going to share drinking water with the cows?"

He slanted her a sideways glance, his mouth lifting in a half grin. "It did occur to me to wonder if you'd think of it."

"Pretty hard not to, what with all the cattle prints around the tank." She gave Sadie's damp hide a final swipe and returned the brush to the shelf. "I thought you said you didn't have many cattle?"

"No, I said I have no clue how many cattle I've got." Jackson tossed the feed sack over the top rail of a stall and untied Sadie. "I haven't had time to count them."

"Oh, that's right." Rebecca took her knapsack out of the saddlebag and waited as Jackson led Sadie down the wide center aisle, pushed open the door and turned her loose in the corral. He walked back to where she stood and hung the halter on a post with others.

"The crew's up at the house having lunch," he commented as they set off across the quiet yard. "Are you hungry?"

"Yes, I am," Rebecca replied, surprised to find it was true. She often opted for yogurt and a cup of coffee at her desk between appointments, or even forgot to eat lunch. But today, her morning had started earlier than normal and had been followed by hours of exercise, leaving her ravenous, despite the snack she'd eaten several hours before.

"The men throw together sandwiches for lunch," Jackson explained, holding the screen door wide. "Nothing fancy. Hank cooks at night, but everybody makes their own meal at noon."

Rebecca nodded, wondering if he thought she'd expected to be served meals three times a day. They walked down the hallway and entered the kitchen.

"Hey, Rebecca." Gib grinned at her, the glass of milk in his hand paused halfway to his lips. "How was your ride?"

"Lovely." Rebecca dropped into the chair that Jackson held for her. He had an ingrained, old-fashioned courtesy that was charming and it never failed to surprise her. He took the chair on her right and began to assemble a sandwich, taking bread from an opened plastic bag before passing it to her. "Thank you," she said automatically.

"Didn't happen to notice any downed fences while you were riding, did you?" Hank asked.

"No, I didn't." Rebecca realized that Jackson had already assembled a sandwich stacked twice the size of hers. "I didn't see any cattle, either, although there were lots of hoofprints at the watering tank."

"Yeah, we see a lot of prints, but rarely see cows. Those cattle are wild as deer." Hank drained his glass and stood. Gib and Mick lingered, though their plates were bare and glasses empty.

"How did you like riding Sadie?" Mick asked.

"She's a sweetheart, with an easy gait and an even temper." Rebecca glanced at him, then down at the mustard she was spreading over a slice of bread, refusing to respond to the wink he gave her.

"She's a quarter horse." Hank's comment rang with pride.

Rebecca glanced up, smiling at his pleased expression. He seemed startled by her good humor, then he frowned at her as if reminded that he didn't want to indulge in pleasant conversation with a woman. He turned his back and stomped across the linoleum-covered floor to the sink, loudly clattering dishes as he rinsed them and put them in the drying rack.

He turned and glared at Gib and Mick. "Ain't you two done yet?"

"Uh, yeah," Gib mumbled. He cast an apologetic glance at Rebecca and shoved back his chair, followed by Mick.

Under Hank's sharp stare, the two rinsed their dishes and put them in the rack.

"See you at dinner, Rebecca," Gib called as they left the kitchen.

"Have a good afternoon," she responded, smiling at the friendly young man, her expression more reserved when she returned Mick's wide grin.

"Don't encourage them."

"What?" Startled, she glanced quickly sideways to find Jackson watching her, his expression grim.

"Don't encourage them," he repeated. "They're already practically standing on their heads to get your attention. Don't make it worse."

"You make them sound like eight-year-olds."

"That's about right."

"Oh, for heaven's sake." Rebecca set down her water glass with a snap. "You make me sound like some sort of femme fatale, trying to lure every man in my vicinity into competing for me."

"You don't need to try. You're the only female in a house full of men." His eyes narrowed. "Don't you have any brothers?"

"No. I'm an only child."

"I should have guessed," he muttered. "Just take my word for it. Don't smile at them." He shoved back his chair and stood.

Rebecca stared at his broad back, nearly speechless with disbelief. "Are you telling me that I'm not allowed to respond to perfectly normal social conversation?"

"No." He rinsed his dishes and stacked them on the rack before turning to look at her. "Just stop smiling at them."

"That's ridiculous."

"Maybe. But you'll avoid a hell of a lot of complications if you try a little harder to discourage those two." And with that, he left the room.

Rebecca glared at the empty doorway, listening to the thud of his boots against the wooden floor, then the slap of the screen door closing.

"That man is insufferable," she muttered before she picked up her sandwich, determined not to let him ruin her lunch.

When nothing was left on her plate but crumbs, she ran soapy water in the sink and quickly washed and stacked the dishes before leaving the kitchen for the office. Here, she booted up the computer and typed a scathing e-mail to her mother telling her all the reasons why Jackson Rand was completely impossible to deal with. Then she hit Delete and erased the message. Feeling much better, not to mention much calmer, she pulled up the ranch account, located her journal-entry file and composed an entry delineating her observances during the morning's ride over the pastures.

Her work on the computer was finished in less than an hour. Considering her options for the rest of the afternoon, Rebecca wandered into the kitchen. She pulled open a cabinet door to take down a mug for tea, and the sight of Hank's "Montana State Fair" mug reminded her that she'd planned to woo his friendship with double-fudge brownies. She closed the door, turned off the burner under the teakettle and went upstairs to collect her purse to drive to town.

Two hours later, she was back in the kitchen. After emptying the grocery bags and stirring up ingredients, she scraped the dark chocolate batter from a mixing bowl into a pan. While the brownies baked, she put together the ingredients for fudge frosting, and by the time Hank entered the kitchen through the back door in late afternoon, the brownies were cooled, frosted and arranged on a plate.

Hank sniffed, his nostrils flaring, and his habitual suspicious expression slowly faded to astonishment.

"Hello, Hank." Rebecca glanced at him and concentrated on washing the last sticky pan at the sink, while casting glances at him through her lashes.

"What smells so good?"

"I baked brownies this afternoon." She rinsed the baking pan and set it in the rack. "I had a craving for chocolate." She squeezed out the sponge and ran it over the already clean countertop, aware that Hank crossed the kitchen and stopped in front of the plate of brownies. "Do you like chocolate, Hank? Those are double fudge, with extra fudge frosting."

"Yeah. I like chocolate."

She tossed the sponge in the sink and looked directly at him. The dazed, yearning expression on his face made her want to laugh out loud, but she quickly swallowed the bubble of laughter.

"I haven't tasted them yet, Hank. I'm a little concerned that I might have used too many chocolate chips—I don't have a copy of the recipe with me so I'm hoping that I remembered it correctly. Would you test them for me?"

"I'd be glad to." Hank reached for a chocolate square as he said the words.

The first bite had him closing his eyes, his face reflecting something approaching ecstasy.

Rebecca bit back a smile. "How are they? Too much chocolate?"

"No, no. Can't get too much chocolate." Hank shook his head. "But maybe I should taste another one, just to be sure."

"Good idea."

The second brownie followed the first, disappearing swiftly. "Good, really good," he said sagely, nodding with approval. He shot her a questioning look. "Is this one of those secret family recipes?"

"Not exactly, although my mom loves them as much as I do. But the recipe itself came from a bakery in my neighborhood in San Francisco."

"Humph. They're tasty."

"Do you think the others might like to have them for dessert tonight?"

Hank eyed the dozen or so chocolate squares left on the plate. "Probably," he said, grudgingly. "But they'll be gone in about two seconds."

"Oh, I made more." Rebecca pulled open the cupboard door to reveal a second plate piled high, and saw Hank's eyes light up. "The recipe is double and I love chocolate, so I thought none of them would be wasted."

"Tell you what," Hank confided. "Don't tell the rest of the boys about the second plate, okay?"

"Okay. But why?"

"Because if you do, both plates will be empty. We should save some of them for tomorrow. Seein' as how you love chocolate so much," he added hastily.

"Well, if you think we should…" Rebecca barely got the words out before Hank reached for the plate.

"We'll need to find a place to hide this so they don't find them. Those three can sniff out food from a mile away."

He shot Rebecca a glance full of pure mischief and she laughed.

"Okay. Since you're familiar with hiding places and I'm not, why don't you pick the place. Just be sure to tell me because I definitely need a brownie for breakfast tomorrow morning."

"Done." He held out his hand.

She took his hand and they shared a firm shake of agreement before he disappeared down the basement steps.

Well, that worked well, she thought with a smile. *I'm thinking U.S. ambassadors should be given this recipe. Who knows how many international crises could be avoided if we only used chocolate?*

Hank wasn't the only one charmed by the chocolate. When Hank produced the brownie-laden plate after dinner, Gib and Mick hooted with delight. For a moment, all was quiet while the men chewed, swallowed and immediately reached for more.

"These are great, Rebecca," Gib enthused.

"Best brownies I've had since the last time I was at my sister's in Missoula," Mick vowed, his usual flirting absent.

"Thank you, Mick. I didn't know you had family in Missoula," she commented, sipping her tea and savoring the decadent chocolate.

"A sister."

"Is that where your family lives?"

"No, my folks live in the next county, but my only

sister married a professor last year and moved to the other side of the state. He teaches at the university in Missoula.''

"How interesting. What does he teach?''

"Poetry and literature.''

Gib groaned and grabbed another brownie.

"You don't like poetry and literature, Gib?'' Rebecca asked.

"No,'' he mumbled around a mouthful of chocolate.

"Neither do I,'' Mick interjected. "But Randy isn't a sissy, which is what I pretty much expected when Gracie said she was bringing home a guy that teaches poetry classes.''

Jackson couldn't remember the last time he'd had home-baked brownies, or anything else, for that matter. No wonder the other three men were falling over themselves to be nice to her. He'd consider buying her flowers in exchange for a promise of a pan of the chocolate squares that were exclusively his, but didn't dare. He had the uneasy feeling that any move by either of them would have them in bed together.

She was too good to be true and it irritated the hell out of Jackson, because he didn't want to like her. He was already struggling with a powerful urge to lure her into the hayloft and find out if she tasted as good as she looked. The growing desire was made worse by the knowledge that she wasn't indifferent to him. Despite the fact that she pointedly used the word

fiancé during conversations, he knew he wasn't misreading the heat that flared between them. He had a
strict rule about not pursuing married or engaged
women—he didn't do it, ever. But Rebecca Parrish
Wallingford was testing his willpower to the breaking
point.

It didn't help that the rest of the men were apparently oblivious to Jackson's problem. Friday night after dinner, Hank stopped him on his way into the
kitchen with a declaration that stunned him.

"I think we should ask Rebecca to join the poker
game tonight."

Jackson stared at Hank and bit back a groan. "Are
you crazy?"

"No, I ain't crazy." Hank looked seriously offended.

"She's a woman," Jackson said patiently. "You
don't like women, remember? You especially don't
like women around when you're playing poker for
money."

"We're only playing for dimes."

Hank's stubborn expression had Jackson shaking
his head. "I give up. Ask her if you want to, but don't
complain if she ruins the game." He spoke the last
few words to Hank's back as the older man headed
for the living room where Rebecca had settled in with
a book.

The two returned just as Gib and Mick were pulling

out chairs at the table and emptying their pockets, dumping coins onto the table in front of them.

"Hey, Rebecca." Gib dropped into his chair and broke the seal on a new deck of cards.

Jackson couldn't fault the friendly smile she gave Gib in return, for there was nothing beyond good nature in her attitude.

"Are you two ready to lose all your dimes?" she asked, lifting a questioning eyebrow to include Mick.

"Yeah, right," Mick scoffed, grinning at her. "I hope you brought your wallet, lady."

Jackson noted that Mick's expression held none of his usual sharp interest in a pretty female.

Hank pulled out a chair for Rebecca and took the seat next to her, leaving her to sit down and tuck her chair closer to the table all by herself. Much to Jackson's surprise, neither Hank nor Gib leaped up to offer their aid, in fact, all three men acted as if she were one of the guys.

It's downright amazing, he thought as he took the vacant chair at the end of the table. She'd somehow managed to stop Gib and Mick from strutting like two roosters in front of the only hen in the house, and convinced Hank to accept her. Jackson was pretty sure that she'd won Hank over with the chocolate brownies. Hank's Achilles' heel was his sweet tooth, although just how Rebecca had figured that out in the short time she'd known him, Jackson had no idea. But what she'd done to convince Gib and Mick to treat her like a sister, now that was a real mystery.

Sure that they were going to have fun teaching Rebecca to play poker and teasing her, the four men quickly discovered that she didn't need lessons.

"Where did you learn to play poker like that?" Hank grumbled as Rebecca took her third pot in an hour.

"From my mom." Rebecca swept the pile of dimes from the center of the table and began to stack them in front of her. "When I was a little girl, most of my friends watched Disney videos when they had a cold and were bored. But Mom and I played poker."

"She turned you into a card shark," Mick complained as he shuffled the deck and began to deal.

"She was good, but Andy was even better."

"Who's Andy? Your brother?" Hank picked up his cards and squinted at them.

"No, unfortunately, I'm an only child. Andy was the chauffeur for my stepfather, Harold. We used to play poker while we waited for Mom and Harold to finish meetings. Andy picked me up at school first, then drove to Mom and Harold's office building. Sometimes we'd wait for an hour or so and we played cards to pass the time." Rebecca finished stacking the coins and picked up her cards, deftly shifting them, lips pursing as she considered her hand.

Jackson eyed her in disbelief. "You had a chauffeur?"

"Not me, personally. He was my stepfather's chauffeur."

"What exactly does your stepfather do?" Mick asked.

"He was a venture capitalist. He owned the company I work for, Bay Area Investments."

"Was?" Jackson asked.

"He passed away a few years ago. My mother took over as CEO, so I work for her now."

"She's probably pretty good at running a company if she can play poker," Hank commented. He tossed a red chip into the center of the table. "Ante up, everybody. I plan to win this hand."

Chapter Four

The Friday-night poker party was the first of many. Rebecca was satisfied that she was establishing a friendly bond with all the men at the Rand Ranch, except for Jackson. Unfortunately, he was the one that she had the most contact with, for each evening after dinner, they worked together in the office. Checking financial data had never been so torturous for her. She found it safer to limit their conversations to work-connected issues and carefully steered clear of any personal comments in an effort to maintain a polite distance between them.

Despite her best efforts, she was unable to ignore the powerful attraction that made her heart beat faster and her temperature rise until she felt her cheeks flush. Sometimes she thought she was succeeding in her campaign to hide her reaction from him. But other times, when she glanced up and caught him watching her from across the room, his eyes hot and intent, she knew very well that she was kidding herself. The sexual tension between them shortened her breath and made her heart pound until he looked away, leaving her feeling singed and restless.

Much to her surprise, the novelty of having free time didn't wear off as she'd expected. Instead, she found herself falling into a regular pattern of waking early, riding Sadie out over the pastures that grew increasingly familiar, then returning to the ranch house for lunch. In the afternoons, she worked at her laptop on the Rand Ranch account and several other files in Bay Investments' home office that she was monitoring long-distance. She frequently drove into Colson, often stopping at Victoria's office to relay a question or message from her mother. Their professional relationship quickly grew into friendship.

Late one morning, she drove to Colson to meet Victoria for lunch, an appointment made two days prior when they'd bumped into each other in the drugstore's cosmetics section.

Rebecca parked in front of Annie's Cafe, the restaurant she'd visited on her first trip to town. Hoping she wouldn't run into the same older woman who'd questioned her the last time she'd been at the Cafe, she pushed open the plate-glass door and walked inside. The air-conditioned interior was blessedly cool after the midday heat on the street.

The Cafe was busy, the booths, tables and counter stools nearly filled with lunch customers. Rebecca scanned the crowded restaurant, smiling when she saw Victoria waving at her from a booth near the back.

She wound her way around the busy tables and dropped onto the upholstered bench seat opposite Victoria.

"Whew, it's packed in here."

"This is Colson's version of rush hour." Victoria's blue eyes lit with amusement. "It takes a little getting used to for us city girls."

"Us city girls? Aren't you a native Colsonite?"

"Heavens, no. I was born and raised in Seattle."

"Then you're a long way from home," Rebecca commented, curious. "How did you end up here?"

"My uncle, aunt and cousin live here. When I was a child, I spent summers visiting them and a few years ago, when I had to leave Seattle because of allergies, I came to Colson."

"And you liked it so much, you stayed," Rebecca guessed.

"Actually, I fell in love with Quinn Bowdrie, married him and stayed."

"Are you happy? Not being married to Quinn," Rebecca went on hastily. "I meant are you happy living in such a small, rural town after growing up in a city as cosmopolitan as Seattle.''

"Strangely enough, yes.'' Victoria's face was pensive. ''It was definitely a culture shock at first, but now there are a thousand things I'd miss if I moved back to the city.''

Rebecca thought about her daily rides on Sadie. ''I have to admit that although I miss shopping in San Francisco and having daily access to vanilla lattes at Starbucks, there are things about Montana that I'll miss very much when I go home.''

"Like what?'' Victoria asked, her voice curious.

"Like walking out the front door and having acres and acres of open land to ride over. Like the lack of street noise at night, the sound of birds singing before dawn and no rush-hour traffic when I drive to town for lunch.'' She smiled at the vigorous nods her comments drew from Victoria.

"Yes,'' Victoria agreed. ''Those are exactly the sort of things I love about living in Colson—or out of Colson, since we live on Quinn's ranch.''

Their conversation was interrupted by the young waitress, who took their orders for the day's special of mixed-greens salad and half of a roast beef sandwich.

"So you're enjoying staying out at Jackson Rand's place?'' Victoria queried when the waitress left.

Rebecca thought a moment. ''Yes, I am.''

"You sound surprised.'' Victoria laughed.

"I am, actually," Rebecca said dryly. "It was dicey at first, and I wasn't sure how comfortable it was going to be sharing a house with four men who were complete strangers. But now, even Hank has stopped frowning at me."

"You're kidding." Victoria looked impressed. "How in the world did you manage that?"

Rebecca smiled, her lips curving with mischief. "Chocolate brownies. Hank's a pushover for chocolate."

Victoria laughed out loud. "No kidding. If I'd known that, I'd have fed him chocolate months ago. He's the perfect age for Nikki's Aunt Cora, and we've been trying to strike up an acquaintance with him ever since he and Jackson Rand came to town. But whenever I say hello to him, he just scowls and grunts hello, then stomps off."

"That sounds like Hank." Rebecca shook her head. "Jackson warned me that he doesn't like women, not women in particular, just women in general."

"Did Jackson tell you why?" Victoria shifted back to let the waitress transfer plates from a tray to the table in front of her.

"No." Rebecca moved her tumbler filled with ice water to one side and smiled her thanks at the waitress before picking up her fork.

"How about Jackson?"

Rebecca glanced up from her salad. "What about Jackson?"

Victoria lifted an eyebrow. "What's he like? Ever since he inherited the ranch after Eli passed away, I've been curious about him. But he doesn't socialize very much. Quinn says he's rebuilding the ranch and doing the work of ten men. The only gossip I've heard about him is from the few comments that his crew has dropped when they're drinking at the Crossroads on a Saturday night. And you know how men are, they never tell the really interesting stuff. Half the women in town are dying to get to know him and here you are, actually living in the same house."

"We have a working relationship," Rebecca protested. "It's not as if I'm dating him."

"Yes, but you're inhabiting the same space, twenty-four hours a day. Come on, Rebecca, tell me what he's like."

Rebecca couldn't help but laugh at Victoria's mischievous smile and twinkling eyes. "I'm not sure I can tell you anything you don't already know. Hmm, let me see." She thought a moment. "He seems completely focused on getting the ranch up and running. As you said, he works very long hours. He's an excellent horseman. He likes to play poker and he's really quite good at it." She paused, trying to think of something personal about Jackson that she could tell Victoria. She wasn't about to tell her that the man was sexy as sin and just being in the same room with him made her think of dark nights and naked bodies.

Victoria waited expectantly but Rebecca couldn't think of anything to tell her that wasn't X-rated. "That's it?" she said finally, lifting an eyebrow in disbelief.

"I'm trying to think of something that you'd be interested in," Rebecca protested, feeling her face heat.

"Is he dating anybody? Has he been married? Divorced? Widowed? Any children? Does he have family—sisters, brothers?"

"Goodness." Rebecca bought time by taking a long drink of ice water. "I don't think he's dating anyone, at least, he hasn't mentioned it and neither have the others. I'm guessing that they'd comment and they'd definitely tease him if he had a woman friend." She frowned, thinking about Victoria's questions and, for the first time, she realized how very little she knew about Jackson. She'd been so focused on maintaining her poise when she was with him that they'd exchanged very little personal information. She knew more about Hank, Gib and Mick than she did about Jackson.

Victoria shook her head. "You're letting the sisterhood of single women down, Rebecca."

Rebecca laughed. "Uh-oh, that's not good."

"No, it's not. I'm going to have to assign you an investigative mission on behalf of the single women of Colson.'' Victoria lifted her glass of ice water and grinned.

''I'm not sure I'd make a good investigator,'' Rebecca said dubiously.

''Sure you will.'' Victoria leaned closer, lowering her voice. ''You just need to focus on finding out everything you can about Jackson Rand—whether he was involved with anyone in the town where he lived before moving to Colson, if he's ever been married or has children and anything else about his personal life that you can discover. Oh,'' Victoria added with relish. ''And we really need to know what his favorite foods are, because Angie Connelly is the best cook among the local single women and she would give free meals to anyone who gave her the inside scoop.''

''I don't know what his favorite foods are, but he definitely likes double-chocolate brownies,'' Rebecca commented, remembering the speed with which Jackson had downed several of the squares she'd baked to charm Hank.

''Aha! Good to know.'' Victoria tilted her glass in acknowledgment of the information.

Rebecca laughed. ''You make it sound as if the local women are planning a battle campaign.''

''Trust me, they are,'' Victoria said. ''Single guys as good-looking as Jackson aren't that plentiful in Colson. This is definitely an important issue.''

''Does your husband know that you're checking

out the local single guys?'' Rebecca asked with a smile.

''Oh, yes,'' Victoria said airily, waving a dismissing hand. ''But he knows I'm only doing it for friends. Oh—'' she stopped abruptly, put down her fork and reached for her purse ''—I have new pictures of Quinn and Sarah.'' She rummaged in her purse and extracted a sheaf of snapshots to hand to Rebecca. ''These were taken last week at Cully and Nikki's house.''

Rebecca accepted the small stack of four-by-six photos, smiling at the first shot of Victoria's little girl, Sarah. ''How old did you say Sarah is?'' she asked.

''She's three. Isn't she cute? My sister-in-law, Nikki's Aunt Cora, knitted that little blue sweater she's wearing.''

''She's adorable,'' Rebecca agreed, moving to the next photo of the little girl playing with a big dog.

''Are you and your fiancé planning to have children?''

''Oh, yes.'' Rebecca nodded. ''As soon as possible.''

''When are you getting married?''

''We haven't set a date yet. We're trying to find a time that fits with both of our schedules, and that's proving to be difficult.'' She slipped the photo behind the others. The new photo was of Victoria sitting on a man's lap, with Sarah in her arms. Victoria and Sarah were laughing at the camera, but the black-haired man in jeans and white T-shirt was looking at the two of them. His expression held such naked adoration that Rebecca caught her breath. She glanced up at Victoria. "This must be your husband?"

"Where?" Victoria tilted her head to see the photo and a soft, warm smile lit her face. "Yes, that's Quinn."

"What a happy family."

"It's easy to be deliriously happy when you find the right person." Victoria took the photo and ran the tip of her fingertip in a circle around the three figures. "Don't you think so?"

Rebecca didn't have an answer. She'd picked Steven carefully from the circle of her acquaintances, but he'd never looked at her with anything approaching the love she saw on the face of Victoria's husband in the photo. She and Steven certainly weren't unhappy, but were they deliriously happy together? Settled, certainly. Comfortable, beyond a doubt. But she didn't think the words "deliriously happy" applied to her and Steven's relationship.

And before Victoria asked the question, it hadn't occurred to her to wonder if being deliriously happy was possible in a man-woman relationship. Nor if that kind of happiness was something that she ought to look for or expect in a marriage.

"Rebecca?"

Rebecca looked up to find Victoria gazing at her with concern. "I'm just trying to remember if I've ever been deliriously happy with a guy,'' she said wryly.

"You don't feel that way with your fiancé?"

"Not that I can remember." Rebecca looked at the next photo; it was a snapshot of Victoria with Sarah and two men. One was Quinn and the other man looked so much like him that it was startling. "Who's this?"

Victoria tilted her head to look at the photo. "That's Cully, Quinn's younger brother." The affection in her voice was echoed by a fond smile that curved her lips.

"They look so much alike," Rebecca commented, slipping the photo to the bottom of the stack. The next snapshot was of Victoria and Quinn seated on a sofa. Sarah was perched on Victoria's lap and a young girl with a mischievous grin, coal-black hair and dark brown eyes, sat on the far side of Quinn, her arm around his shoulder. "Who's this little girl?"

"Quinn and Cully's little half sister, Angelica. They share the same father but Angelica had a different mother." Victoria pointed at the next photo. "This is Nikki, Angelica's half sister on her mother's side. She's married to Cully and Angelica lives with them."

Confused, Rebecca frowned. "Excuse me? Angelica's half sister is married to her half brother?"

Victoria laughed, her eyes twinkling. "Nikki and Cully aren't related to each other, only to Angelica.

Nikki and Angelica share a mother and Cully and Angelica share a father, but there's absolutely no blood connection between Nikki and Cully.''

"Goodness, that's confusing," Rebecca commented. The woman in the photo with her arm around Cully's waist had auburn hair and velvety dark eyes. There was an aura of contentment and happiness about them. She glanced up at Veronica. "Are she and Cully deliriously happy, like you and Quinn?"

"Yes." Victoria's smile was warm. "Although there was a time when I doubted they'd work things out between them. Nikki was in love with Cully when I married Quinn, but it was only after Angelica was seriously ill that they finally got together. I'm still not certain exactly what happened four years ago, but it was serious. Nikki moved to Seattle for several years and didn't return until Angelica became so ill."

"What happened? Was it serious?"

"Yes. She had aplastic anemia, a rare blood disease. Cully saved her life by donating bone marrow."

"Oh my." Rebecca could only shake her head in sympathy at Victoria's comment. It occurred to her that she'd led a relatively secure existence, with no serious health issues in her family and no broken hearts. "Is Angelica fully recovered?" She glanced at Victoria for confirmation as she held out the photos.

"Yes, thank goodness." Victoria took the stack of photos from Rebecca's outstretched hand.

"It must be wonderful to be part of a large family," Rebecca commented as Victoria tucked the photos back in her purse.

"It is," Victoria confirmed. "But it can be very noisy when we're all together for holidays, birthdays, etcctcra."

"I've always wished I had brothers or sisters, cousins or aunts and uncles." Rebecca picked up her fork and took a bite of her salad.

"You're an only child?" Victoria asked.

"Yes."

"But surely you have other relatives? Were your mother and father only children, also?"

"Apparently." Rebecca, uncomfortable with discussing her unknown father, changed the subject. Fortunately, Victoria followed her lead without comment.

They parted after lunch with a promise to get together soon.

Two days after her lunch with Victoria, Rebecca was alone in the house on Saturday night. Hank, Gib and Mick had already left, planning to meet friends for their regular, twice-monthly night of poker playing. Jackson was still working, repairing a fence in one of the distant pastures. Rebecca hadn't seen him since early morning, when he'd packed a lunch and she'd overheard him telling Hank not to delay dinner for him since he had no idea exactly when he'd be home.

Rebecca curled up on the sofa, turned on the television and tuned in the programming channel, searching for a movie on the schedule that looked interesting before going to the kitchen to find something for dinner.

She'd narrowed her choices down to a rerun of Harrison Ford in *Raiders of the Lost Ark* or Deborah Kerr and Cary Grant in *An Affair to Remember.* While Harrison was eminently watchable, she thought she might prefer the more traditional romance with Grant and Kerr.

"Hmm, a two-hanky movie with Cary Grant or a roller-coaster action trip with Harrison? Decisions, decisions," she murmured aloud. She'd nearly decided to flip a coin when she heard the door off the utility room slap shut. A short moment later, Jackson paused in the living-room doorway.

"Where is everybody?"

His jeans and boots were smudged with dust, his shirt just as dirty and ripped at the shoulder, and his cheekbone was highlighted with a smear of black that looked like oil or grease.

"They drove into Colson. Hank said to tell you to join them if you want. They're at Joe-somebody's house playing poker."

"Joe never has any food except beer, peanuts and potato chips. I feel like having a steak. Have you eaten?"

"No." She uncurled her legs and rose from the

sofa. "But I was about to raid the refrigerator. The guys were going to grab something in town, and I was just trying to decide what to eat when you came in."

He ran his fingers through his hair, raking it back off his forehead, his gaze unreadable. "Why don't you get dressed and come into town with me. I'll buy us a steak."

"It's lovely of you to offer, Jackson, but I don't think…"

"Part of my contract with Bay Investments requires that I provide three meals a day for their financial representative. That's you."

"I know, but that doesn't mean that you have to buy me a meal."

"Humor me," he interrupted her. "I'm tired and hungry. Keep me company."

"Well, I…" Rebecca said dubiously. Sharing a meal in the ranch house kitchen was one thing, but going out to eat seemed a bit too much like a date. And she wasn't going to date Jackson. Not that he'd asked, she reminded herself. But spending the evening in the empty house with Jackson seemed just as chancy. On the other hand, her luncheon conversation with Victoria had made her aware of the fact that she was avoiding Jackson.

"I don't bite, Rebecca." His mouth quirked in a half grin. "And you're an engaged woman so you're perfectly safe with me."

There was no concealing the fact that his drawled comment was a thinly veiled dare. Rebecca might acknowledge to herself that she'd been avoiding him. But she was damned if she would let him believe avoidance meant that she was afraid to spend time with him.

"Very well." She walked toward him. "I hope you plan to change your clothes?"

The cool glance she gave him only elicited a half smile. He turned his hands palms up and considered the dirt. "Yes, ma'am. I'll take a shower first."

"Excellent." She paused and glanced at her watch. "I'll be ready in thirty minutes."

"Good." He stood aside and gestured toward the stairs. "The sooner we're out of here, the sooner we'll have that steak."

Rebecca walked past him, up the stairs and down the hall. She was intensely aware of him walking behind her, and when she reached her bedroom and stepped inside, she closed the door and sagged back against it. In the bathroom next door, the shower came on, the sound of water hitting the tiled wall drowning out her deep breaths.

Jackson always seemed to suck the oxygen out of the air, she thought as she pushed away from the door. She instinctively knew that it was dangerous to go anywhere with him; in fact, she wasn't sure she should change her tactic of avoid and retreat. But she wasn't a child and it annoyed her to think he might assume that she was intimidated by him.

She moved hangers aside in the closet and pulled out the black cocktail dress that she always packed for business trips. She tossed it on the bed and stripped off her khaki shorts and white tank top. Twenty minutes later, she was dressed, fresh makeup applied, her hair brushed into a sleek ebony fall that curved under and brushed her shoulders. Her black sandals had three-inch heels and it occurred to her that she didn't need to worry about towering over Jackson. She never wore this particular pair of shoes with Steven, who complained that these shoes made her taller than his five feet ten inches.

Exactly thirty minutes after she'd climbed the stairs, Rebecca descended them to find Jackson in the hallway below, waiting for her. Her nerves tightened when his gaze swept over her from her hair to her sandal-shod feet, making the return trip with a slow thoroughness. His gold eyes were so hot that she felt scorched, her own temperature rising, and she felt a swift panic that she might be out of her depth.

Then his lashes lowered, concealing his expression, and he glanced at his watch. "Thirty minutes exactly. I don't think I've ever met a woman who could be ready to go somewhere on time."

He pushed away from the wall where he'd been leaning and held open the screen door.

"Maybe you haven't met the right sort of women."

Rebecca walked past him, the scent of soap mingled with aftershave reaching her nostrils.

"That could be," he conceded mildly.

She moved ahead of him down the walk to the open gate and the yard beyond where his truck was parked. He reached around her to open the passenger door and held it wide. Rebecca looked at the height of the seat, then down at her skirt and realized that she couldn't climb into the cab without hiking her skirt up around her waist. And that wasn't even a remote possibility in front of Jackson.

Just as she was about to explain her problem, Jackson solved the situation by picking her up and lifting her onto the seat, his hands nearly encircling her waist.

Startled, she had to catch her breath before she could speak. "Thank you."

"No problem." He closed the door and walked around the front of the truck. By the time he slid beneath the wheel, Rebecca had fastened her seat belt and drawn several deep breaths to calm her racing pulse.

"Where are we going to have dinner?" she asked as he started the truck and shifted into gear.

"The Crossroads in Colson."

"The Crossroads? I thought it was a bar."

"It is. Actually, there's a bar in one half of the building and a restaurant in the other. The cook grills the best steaks this side of Miles City."

She glanced at him, dubious. "Is that good?"

His mouth curved in a smile. "That's very good. I don't know what secret recipe Kenny uses, but the steaks are excellent."

"I'm not a big fan of large slabs of red meat."

Jackson laughed. "Don't say that to just anybody, honey, this is cattle country and most of the ranchers in the county make a living selling beef. They might take offense if you turned up your nose at beefsteak."

"I'll try to remember not to tell anyone that I prefer chicken and vegetables," she said dryly, charmed by the teasing smile he gave her.

A half hour later, Jackson turned into the parking lot of the Crossroads Bar and Grill. The gravel lot was packed with pickup trucks and cars, but he expertly wedged the big truck between two cars in a far corner. Rebecca unfastened her seat belt and reached for the door latch.

"Wait, I'll help you out."

She obeyed, steeling herself for the brush of her body against his when he lifted her down. But he didn't swing her to the ground. Instead, he cradled her in his arms, shoved the door closed with his elbow and set off across the lot toward the concrete-block building. Instinctively, she closed her hand over the slope of his shoulder and the hard muscles flexed beneath her palm and fingers.

"I can walk," she protested.

"The gravel will ruin those pretty shoes." He

glanced down at her, then away, and her heartbeat stuttered. He was much too close, the heat of his body branding hers down one side, the powerful muscles of his arms beneath her knees and around her back flexing as he strode across the uneven lot.

They reached the paved walkway that ran around the perimeter of the building, and Jackson lowered her to her feet. She swayed, momentarily disoriented, and caught his forearm to steady her equilibrium.

"Are you all right?" He waited until she nodded yes before pulling open the heavy glass door and ushering her into the building. The wide hallway had a door to their right with a neon sign arched above it proclaiming "Grill." Ahead of them, at the end of the hall, a similar door on the left read "Bar." The sound of country-and-western music came from the far door, the heavy thump of the bass an underlying note to the murmur of voices and laughter.

"It's Saturday night," Jackson commented. "Looks like the Crossroads has a crowd." He held open the door to the Grill.

They stepped into the air-conditioned restaurant and joined a line of three other couples waiting to be seated. The hostess was quick and efficient, but in the few moments they waited, Rebecca was deeply aware of Jackson's broader body standing close behind her. The heat he generated reached out and warmed her, and each time he moved, she caught a faint scent of soap and aftershave mixed with the unique scent that was his alone. Her skin felt hypersensitive and critically attuned to each movement he made.

At last, the hostess led them to a booth near the back of the restaurant. Rebecca slid onto the cool, brown leather-upholstered bench with relief, for it placed the width of the table between her and Jackson.

She opened her menu and spent a moment scanning the dinner offerings. Across from her, Jackson sat at ease, his menu untouched at the edge of the table.

"What are you having?" she asked.

"A New York steak, baked potato, green beans and apple pie with ice cream."

Rebecca laughed. "You're clearly a man who doesn't need the menu."

"Nope. I've been thinking about dinner for the last six hours, ever since I dropped my lunch into the water trough."

"Goodness. How did that happen?"

"You don't want to know."

The waitress appeared, carrying two tall glasses of ice water. After depositing the moisture-beaded cold glasses on the tabletop in front of them, she smiled invitingly at Jackson, pencil poised above an order pad. "What can I get you folks this evening?"

Jackson ignored the woman's flirting and lifted a questioning eyebrow at Rebecca, who smiled and closed her menu. "I'll live dangerously tonight. I'll have what you're having."

"Good choice." He gave their order to the waitress and she departed.

Despite the waitress's obvious interest, he hadn't seemed to even notice, Rebecca thought.

"So, now that you've been here for a few weeks, how do you feel about being so far from San Francisco?" Jackson asked. "Are you missing the ballet and opera yet?"

"No. But the opera and ballet season won't start until fall. Maybe by then, I'll miss them." Rebecca smiled sunnily back when he narrowed his eyes at her.

"How about shopping? Don't women love to shop?"

"Sure, but I can shop in Colson."

He looked distinctly unbelieving. "It's hard to believe that you don't miss something about the city."

"I miss vanilla lattes at Starbucks," she said promptly. "But there are lots of things I don't miss about San Francisco that I really enjoy about Montana."

"Really? Like what?"

She repeated what she'd told Victoria about how much she enjoyed riding Sadie across the open pastureland, hearing birds singing before dawn, the lack of traffic and street noise. The subject reminded her that Victoria had teased her about finding out information regarding Jackson's background, so she ended her list with a question. "What about you? Do you miss the town you lived in before you came to Colson?''

"No." He shrugged. "But then, it was about the same size."

"Not a big city?"

"No. Definitely not a big city." His mouth curved with amusement. "In fact, I doubt the population of Haydons Creek is as large as Colson."

"Haydons Creek? Is that in Montana?"

"Yes, in the Judith Basin."

"And what did you do there?" Rebecca sipped her water and eyed him, her gaze running over muscled forearms, tanned a dark brown below the turned-back cuffs of his white shirt, and the faint pale lines radiating from the corner of his eyes. "I'm guessing that you didn't work in an office?"

He laughed, the corners of his eyes crinkling. "No, I didn't. I ran a cattle ranch for an absentee landlord."

"Have you always been a rancher?"

"Yes, all my life. I never wanted to do anything else. What about you? Have you always been a financial officer?"

"Yes. I went to work for my stepfather's firm directly out of college and I've been there ever since."

"Never wanted to do anything else?"

Rebecca laughed. "When I was a little girl, I wanted to be lots of things. Everything from a ballerina to the president of the United States."

"I'm surprised you settled for something so ordinary.'' His smile was warm, friendly, and Rebecca felt herself relaxing.

''As I grew older, I became more practical,'' she confessed. ''It made sense to go into the family business. Besides, my stepfather was much older than Mom and I knew she'd be running Bay Investments by herself one day. I wanted to work with her and, since I'm an only child, she warned me that I needed a lot of background experience in all phases of the company in order to take over when she retires.''

''So you're an heiress?''

''Of sorts.'' She shook her head at the faintly cynical twist of his lips. ''But it's more work and responsibility than anything else.'' She narrowed her eyes. ''And don't give me that look. You're an heir, so you know very well that there's a burden of responsibility that makes the money secondary.''

''I'm Eli's heir,'' he agreed. ''But there was very little money involved, that's why I took a loan from Bay Investments. I inherited a lot of land and very little else.''

''But the land is very valuable, so in a sense, there *is* a lot of money involved.''

''Yes, but if I sold the land to get the money, then I wouldn't have a ranch to spend the money on, and I can't see myself lying on a beach somewhere, doing nothing for the rest of my life.''

Rebecca couldn't argue with his logic. ''It's really a catch-22, isn't it?''

"Pretty much." The waitress arrived with their food and Jackson leaned back to allow her to move plates from tray to tabletop.

"This looks wonderful," Rebecca commented. Her steak wasn't the huge chunk of rare beef that she'd expected. Fresh green beans accompanied the steaming baked potato.

"It tastes better. Try it."

Jackson waited until she sliced a small bit of the steak and popped it in her mouth.

"You're right," she said after swallowing, surprised at how delicious the steak was. "This is excellent."

"I heard that Kenny was a chef in Seattle when he was younger. People tell me that the fish here is as good as the steak, but I haven't tried the trout yet."

For moments, conversation was abbreviated as they applied themselves to dinner. Rebecca discovered that she was hungrier than she'd thought and cleared her plate, but she declined Jackson's offer of dessert, opting for coffee only. While he tucked into apple pie with vanilla ice cream, Rebecca returned to their earlier conversation.

"So you can't see yourself selling the ranch, taking the money and living a life of ease. A lot of people would think that's heaven, why not you?"

He shrugged. "I've worked on ranches since I was born. I can't imagine retiring at my age and, besides, I like the life."

"Was your father a rancher?"

"He didn't own his own place, but he worked on ranches all his life. He was a foreman for the Atchison Conglomerate in Wyoming when he died."

"I'm sorry."

"Don't be. It happened when I was twelve and that was a long time ago."

"You were only twelve? But that's so young. Did your mother remarry?"

"My mother died with my dad."

Rebecca caught her breath, her eyes widening. "Oh, Jackson. I never knew my real father, but I have my mother and also had a stepfather until I was in my twenties. How awful that you lost both your parents at once. What happened?"

He pushed aside his empty plate and lifted his coffee cup to his lips. Rebecca couldn't read any sadness in his expression.

"They were driving home from Casper in late December. The roads were icy and the car slid off the road and down an embankment. Both of them were killed instantly."

Rebecca shook her head. "That's terrible. How awful for you. Did you have family in the area, grandparents or aunts and uncles?"

"No. I was an only child of only children. They were older when they had me, and both sets of grandparents died when I was a little kid. I barely remember them."

"But if there were no family members to take you into their home, what happened to you? Who cared for you?"

"What usually happens in that situation—I went into foster care."

Rebecca had read newspaper accounts of horrific foster-care situations in San Francisco. Her heart lurched at his matter-of-fact statement. "Did you have good foster parents?"

"Not that I remember. I kept running away and the cops would find me and take me back. I was fifteen when I was finally smart enough to run to another state, far enough away that they couldn't find me."

"But you were only fifteen—how did you survive?"

"I told a rancher in western Montana that I was eighteen. He believed me and gave me a job. I was always bigger than other kids my age and looked older. I stayed there until my eighteenth birthday, then I joined the army."

"But what about school?" Rebecca knew that similar versions of Jackson's story happened to children all across America, but hearing him give the bare facts of his life from the tender age of twelve was somehow worse for the casual way he told it.

"I studied on my own after I left Wyoming, pretty hit-and-miss, but it was enough to pass the GED test. And I finished a couple years of college in the army."

"But you didn't graduate?"

"No. I probably would have kept taking classes if I'd stayed in the army, but I wanted to come back to Montana. And ranch work is what I love. I didn't need a college degree to run a ranch."

"What an amazing story," she said softly, eyeing him over the rim of her cup. "You truly are a self-made man."

"Not quite," he answered. "I dreamed about owning a ranch someday and saved every penny I could to get there. But if Eli hadn't left me his land, I would never have been able to afford a place with the kind of potential of the Kuhlman spread."

"But just surviving as you did, without any help from family…" She shook her head. "I'm not sure I could have done that."

"I take it you have a lot of family connections—grandparents, aunts, uncles?"

Rebecca returned her cup to its saucer. "No, actually I'm an only child, as well. Except for my mother, I don't have any family as far as I'm aware." She ran her finger around the rim of the cup, staring unseeingly at the cream china. "I always wanted a brother and sister, and I would have loved to have grandparents and aunts, uncles…" She glanced up to find him watching her. "Does it bother you? Being all alone?"

"I don't think about it much, don't have time. I suppose it would be nice to have a family for the holidays."

"I had lunch with Victoria the other day and she had pictures of her husband and daughter, plus a little half sister and her husband's brother and his wife. It made me wonder what it would be like to have a bigger family."

"Won't you get all that when you marry?"

Startled, Rebecca realized she hadn't given a single thought to Steven all night. "Yes, I suppose I will." A mental image of Steven's coolly polite mother and frivolous sister came to mind. "I'm not sure."

"You're not sure?" His expression was quizzical. "Haven't you met your prospective in-laws?"

"Yes, of course. But I'm not sure a person really knows how these relationships will work out until you're actually married."

"You've got that right," he growled.

"Pardon?"

"I said that's true."

"How do you know?"

"I was married."

Chapter Five

"You were married?" Rebecca struggled to conceal her surprise.

"When I was twenty-two." Jackson shook his head in disgust. "Too young and too stupid to know better."

"What happened?"

"She was bored."

Rebecca's mouth dropped open in shock. He laughed and leaned forward to gently tap her chin with his forefinger. "She was my boss's only daughter and spoiled rotten. We both had a bad case of raging hormones and the marriage lasted three months. But during that three months, her mama threw daily fits because her daughter had married beneath her. Needless to say, when the marriage ended, so did my job. Not that I would have stayed,'' he added when Rebecca would have commented. "In fact, I drew my pay and was long gone before the ink was dry on the divorce papers.''

"Have you ever wished it ended differently?"

"I'm not sorry it ended, because we had nothing in common outside the bedroom. There wasn't a chance in hell we would have been happy living together for the rest of our lives. But I suppose I'm sorry that we didn't just have an affair and go our separate ways when it ended instead of getting married.''

"And you've never remarried?"

"No. I learned my lesson. Marriage isn't for me." He eyed her. "How about you? Have you ever been married?"

"No."

"Ever come close before?"

"No." It suddenly occurred to Rebecca that she was growing daily less convinced that she was "close" now. Her conversation with Victoria about husbands and marriage had raised doubts about whether marrying Steven was the right choice.

Abruptly, Jackson drained his coffee cup. "Are you ready to go?"

"Yes." Rebecca collected her purse.

Jackson stood, slid his wallet out of his back jeans

pocket, consulted the tab and tossed several bills atop it. She slipped out of the booth and walked ahead of him to the exit. But when they stepped out of the restaurant and into the hall, Jackson stopped her with a hand at her waist, gently turning her toward the far door leading to the bar.

"Let's check out the band in the bar before we leave."

"Oh, I don't think I…" she protested, her wary senses warning her to end the evening before Jackson's company charmed her further and strengthened her doubts about Steven.

"Come on," he coaxed, urging her down the hallway. "We'll have one drink and then head home."

"Well, I…"

"It's Saturday night. You don't really want to go home early on Saturday night, do you? Or is a cowboy bar too blue-collar for a San Francisco heiress?"

Rebecca stiffened and tilted her chin at him. "Are you suggesting that I'm a snob, Mr. Rand?"

"Not at all, Miss Wallingford. I'm just wondering if you're accustomed to being tucked into bed with milk and cookies at…" he glanced at his watch "…nine o'clock on Saturday night." He shrugged. "But it's your call."

"A glass of wine sounds quite good, actually." Rebecca spun on her heel and stalked down the hallway. *Milk and cookies.* She fumed. *Is that how he sees me? As a child to be tucked into bed early with milk?*

She reached the double doors beneath the neon ''Bar'' sign but before she could yank it open, Jackson reached around her and pulled it wide. They stepped inside on a wave of music, laughter and voices. Rebecca halted abruptly and half turned to ask Jackson whether he wanted to sit at the bar or in a booth, and caught sight of their reflection in a mirrored section of wall to their right.

Their images shocked her and held her motionless; she was struck by how culturally different they appeared, yet how much a couple they seemed to be. He was taller than her by several inches, his muscled body clad in white shirt and jeans a perfect contrast to her sophisticated little black dress and slender curves. They were night and day, light and dark, with her raven hair and dark green eyes foils for his brown hair and gold eyes. His hand lay lightly at her waist and, as she watched, he bent his head to whisper in her ear. She shivered at the swift mental image of Jackson naked, kneeling above her, bending to take her mouth with his.

''What's wrong?''

Rebecca jerked her gaze away from the images in the mirror and looked at him. He was much too close, she realized, but the bar was crowded and noisy. He clearly had tried to tell her something, but she wasn't paying attention.

''What?''

He frowned. ''Are you all right?''

"Yes. I'm fine. What did you say?"

"I asked if you want to sit at the bar or in a booth?"

"A booth, I think."

He nodded, his hand leaving her waist to catch hers, tugging her after him as he made a path through the crowd toward the far side of the bar. Rebecca followed, grateful that he was running interference. They reached an unoccupied booth and Jackson released her hand to let her slip onto the seat.

He remained standing. "What kind of wine would you like?"

"Any chablis is fine."

"I'll be right back."

Rebecca watched him move through the crowd and reach the bar. While she waited for him to return, she people-watched. Some of the men were dressed like Jackson, in clean shirts and jeans, while others wore khakis or slacks with dress shirts. The women wore outfits that ranged from tight jeans and western shirts to skirts and blouses. She didn't see anyone in basic black but the mix was so varied that she didn't feel overdressed. The crowd was clearly out to let its hair down and have a good time, and the dance floor was thronged with couples spinning and laughing.

She glanced back at the bar just in time to see Jackson turning toward her, a long-necked beer bottle in one hand and a wineglass in the other. He balanced the drinks and adroitly avoided dancing couples as he walked toward her.

Sharing dinner with him had been a revelation, she thought, for he'd been surprisingly willing to answer her questions about his past. And she'd confided in him, as well, which wasn't usual for her. A private person, Rebecca rarely discussed her family situation with anyone other than her mother and a very few close friends. She had no idea why she'd told Jackson about the responsibility she felt to her mother and Bay Investments, nor about her lack of an extended family and how much she wished it wasn't so. Jackson's ability to draw her out was unique in her experience, and she wasn't sure she was comfortable with it. It was enough that she was physically drawn to him, but to learn that he was the type of person she could connect with on a deeper level was too much to cope with at the moment.

"Here you are." He set the wineglass on the table in front of her and slid into the booth on the opposite bench. He lifted his bottle and drank before gesturing to the crowded dance floor. "What do you think of the residents of Colson?"

"Interesting," she commented, laughing when he quirked an eyebrow at her and grinned. "I'm not sure I know this dance they're doing. What is it?"

"A version of country swing. You've never done it?"

"No. I had lessons that taught me how to waltz, two-step and tango, but not this."

He shook his head, his gold eyes gleaming. "Then we'd better take care of that gap in your education." He caught her hand and stood, pulling her with him out onto the dance floor.

Moments later, Rebecca was trying to follow the music as Jackson twirled her, then tucked her against his side, his arm around her waist as he demonstrated the steps. If she stumbled, he caught her, laughing when he turned one way and she went the other, resulting in her stepping on his boots. He wrapped his arms around her, steadying her before starting again.

By the time the fast-paced song ended, Rebecca was out of breath, as much from laughter as the swift pace. They halted on the dance floor, both chuckling.

"That was so much fun! But I'm so sorry I stepped on your feet."

"I think I'll survive." He glanced down at her feet. "Maybe if you'd stepped on my foot with those heels, I might be complaining."

Rebecca's gaze followed his to her feet, slender and feminine in the spiky-heeled sandals, and then to his much bigger feet in black cowboy boots.

"They can be lethal." She lifted her head and her gaze met his just as the band started playing a slow waltz.

Jackson cocked his head to listen and smiled at her.

''Sounds like a waltz. Since you've had lessons in this, I think my feet are safe.''

Before Rebecca could protest, he slipped his arm around her waist and took her other hand in his.

Her cotillion classes that taught her the waltz hadn't prepared her for waltzing with Jackson. He didn't hold her a decorous twelve inches away; instead, he pulled her close and each smooth step they took together had their bodies brushing, his thigh sliding against hers. The slower music emptied the booths and tables and packed the dance floor with couples, narrowing the space between her and Jackson until she was pressed against him, their steps slowing as space to move was limited even more.

Rebecca was abruptly aware that being held in Jackson's arms, even under the pretext of dancing, threatened her ability to remain immune to him. If she had managed to convince herself that she could ignore the attraction between them by avoiding him, the possibility was blown away by the feel of his arm at her waist and the press of his chest against hers.

His arms tightened, easing her closer, his cheek touching her temple. Rebecca closed her eyes and turned her face against the warm column of his throat. Each breath she drew pulled in the subtle male scents of aftershave, soap and an indefinable flavor that was his alone.

He lifted her hand to rest on his shoulder and slipped his free arm around her waist. Rebecca was

blindsided by the avalanche of tactile pleasure flooding her and only felt relief when both his arms were
wrapped around her waist, holding her closer. Her
hands slipped around his neck, her fingers finding the
soft silk of his hair just above his collar. Pressed
against him from cheek to thigh, Rebecca felt her
bones melting as her breasts tightened and her pulse
pounded. So absorbed was she in her overloaded
senses that she didn't realize the music had ended
until Jackson stopped moving and reluctantly eased a
space between them.

Confused and distracted, she tilted her head back
and her gaze met his. The heat and raw desire in his
eyes snapped the sensual spell that held her, and she
slipped her arms from around his neck and took a
step back, breaking all body contact.

"I think we should go." Her voice was husky from
the desire that pounded through her veins.

Jackson nodded. He waited while she collected her
purse from the booth, then moved toward the door.
He didn't take her hand this time, carefully keeping
a space between them as they slowly worked their
way through the crowd. They were nearly at the exit
when a voice stopped them.

"Jackson! Hey, Jackson."

Rebecca paused, glancing over her shoulder to see
Mick pushing his way through the crowd toward them.

"Mick." Jackson's voice stopped just short of impatient.

"Hey, boss." He grinned at Rebecca. "Hi, Rebecca. Are you two headed for the ranch?"

"Yeah."

"Any chance I can catch a ride with you? Hank drove into town and dropped me off but the guy I was going to ride home with left with his girl."

"Sure. No problem."

Mick didn't seem to pick up on the tension between Jackson and Rebecca, and she was relieved that a third party erased the necessity of conversation on the way home. Mick and Jackson discussed work and she rarely commented.

Driving from Colson to the ranch, Rebecca was wedged between Jackson and Mick in the cab of the truck, the two broad-shouldered men taking up much of the space on the wide bench seat. Pressed snugly against Jackson, she felt branded by the heat of his body down her left side from shoulder to thigh. She reminded herself over and over during the long drive home that she was engaged to Steven, and that any possibility of exploring the passion that blazed between her and Jackson was forbidden. But for the first time in her life, she questioned her decision to ban passion from her life. Could she be missing something vital—something worth chancing the emotional chaos that could result from involvement? Never before had she felt empathy for her mother's situation and the affair that had led to her own birth. In fact, she'd always been baffled by the fact that her pragmatic mother had once been carried away by passion. Now it was all too easy to envision being blinded by sensual appeal.

Sitting next to Rebecca in the truck cab, Jackson barely managed to follow Mick's conversation, distracted by the soft, feminine body next to him. It didn't help that the cab was crowded with the three of them and, as a result, Rebecca was tucked tight against his side. He never should have taken her to the Crossroads for dinner, and he damn sure shouldn't have given in to the reckless urge to dance with her. Instead of easing the ache, holding her while they danced had only made it worse. His brain told him that she was engaged to another man and off-limits, but her every action told him that she didn't love her absent fiancé. He was sure he wasn't misreading the signals she was sending, nor the intensity of the heat that lay between them, despite her obvious determination to ignore it.

He couldn't help but wonder why she'd become engaged to a man she referred to with affection, but never passion.

In the days following their Saturday night at the Crossroads, Rebecca went back to avoiding Jackson. Not that it solved the problem, but she couldn't think of a better solution for her conflicted thoughts and feelings, so she stuck with her original plan, even though it was clear to her that it hadn't a prayer of working.

She wished there were someone she could confide in and discuss her confusion over Jackson and her uncertainty about her engagement to Steven, but she didn't feel ready to tell Victoria and she was equally reluctant to tell her mother, because Kathleen had never been enthusiastic about her choice of Steven as a husband.

It didn't help her mixed feelings that, when she made her customary once-weekly telephone call to Steven, he was heading out the door to catch a plane for a meeting in New York and was too rushed to say more than hello, how are you and goodbye. She hung up feeling even more conflicted about where their relationship was going and whether their marriage would go on as planned.

The temperature climbed steadily higher over the next few days. Rebecca shifted her schedule, saddling Sadie just after dawn and returning to the house before nine o'clock in an effort to avoid the scorching heat later in the morning.

The old house had no air-conditioning and, despite leaving her window wide when she went to bed, Rebecca had difficulty sleeping. Late one night, long after the rest of the house had fallen silent, she stood in front of the open window hoping to catch a cooling breeze. But the night was still, the air inside her room stuffy and much too hot.

On impulse, she grabbed her pillow and pulled the white sheet off the foot of her bed, where she'd long since kicked it and, carrying it over one arm, listened at the door. No sound came from the hall, and she carefully opened the door and slipped through, tiptoeing down the hallway, then the stairs, and out onto the porch.

The night air was several degrees cooler outside the house, whose walls trapped the heat of day inside. Rebecca wrapped the sheet around her, quietly dragged one of the old oak rocking chairs closer to the porch railing and curled up in the wide seat. She propped her feet on the railing, crossed her ankles and gently pushed, setting the rocker moving slowly back and forth.

The moon was three-quarters full, its silvery light turning the ranch and the surrounding pastures and buttes into a mysterious world of black-and-white. Silence reigned, broken occasionally by the sound of raccoons quarreling in the grove of trees at the spring behind the house. Birds stirred and called softly, rustling the leafy upper branches of the old maple tree before settling.

The quiet night eased the restlessness that had disturbed Rebecca's sleep each night since she'd danced with Jackson at the Crossroads. When she did fall asleep, she tossed and turned, victim of dreams that left her waking unsettled.

She knew that her time in Montana was brief, that she would return to her life in San Francisco and it was unlikely that her path would cross Jackson's again. But the yearning she felt for him was a physical ache. The more time she spent in his company, the more she had to stifle the urge to reach out to him. She was drawn to the gentleness she saw when he worked with the horses and to the affectionate, respectful way he treated Hank, making the older man feel an integral part of the heavy workload on the ranch. She wanted to ask her mother if this compulsion to be near him, to touch him, was what her mother had felt toward her biological father, but couldn't bring herself to broach the subject. Her mother had never, ever, talked about her real father, and Rebecca instinctively felt that doing so would be painful for her. The few times she'd asked questions when she was a little girl, her mother had cried. Rebecca had quickly learned not to ask about him.

Sighing, she shifted in the seat, staring broodingly out at the dark landscape.

Behind her, the screen door creaked softly. Startled, she turned her head to see Jackson step onto the porch. He wore only a pair of jeans, his chest and feet bare.

"What are you doing out here in the middle of the night? Are you all right?" He moved toward her, out of the shadow cast by the porch's roof and nearer the railing. The moonlight highlighted his work-sculpted torso, his hair tousled as if he'd been running his fingers through it.

"I'm fine," she answered, her voice hushed. "It was too hot in my bedroom and I couldn't sleep, so I came down here where it's cooler."

"Ah." His muscles loosened and he padded to the railing where he sat sideways, one knee resting on the rail, the other foot planted on the cool boards of the porch. "I'm guessing that it doesn't get this hot in San Francisco?"

"Not at night. We have a few really warm days in the summertime, but usually there's a marine breeze that keeps the city cool."

He nodded. Silence stretched. Neither seemed capable of casual, polite conversation; the dark night seemed somehow private, more intimate.

"Hank told me that you're going to the Fourth of July celebration tomorrow with Victoria Bowdrie," Jackson said at last, breaking the silence.

"Yes. Her husband's family joins Victoria's aunt and uncle and a host of other friends to make a day of it. I'm driving into Colson before lunch."

"The crew is working until noon, then I'm giving them the rest of the day off, so you'll probably run into them at the picnic."

"What about you? Aren't you going?"

"Maybe later, I have some things I need to get done tomorrow."

"You work too hard, Jackson. The world won't come to an end if you take a day off."

He grinned, his teeth flashing against tanned skin. "Maybe not, but if I don't do them tomorrow, they're added to the list for the next day and that list is already too long."

"A rancher's work is never done?"

"Exactly. Especially not this rancher." He looked away from her, toward the dark shapes of the buttes in the distance, and moonlight briefly highlighted the hard bone structure of his face before he turned back to her. "If I finish early, I might drive in later for the barbecue. Hank tells me it's the best free meal all year."

Rebecca laughed. "I've heard the same thing. The beef is barbecued by the men, but all the women in the county bring their best recipes for all the side dishes and desserts. It's evidently an unofficial cooking baking competition."

"A baking competition? Are you taking fudge brownies?"

"No—but I'm sure someone else will bake some."

"Are you staying for the dance after the barbecue?"

"I suppose so—Victoria said not to plan on getting home until late at night."

"Save me a waltz." His voice was suddenly deeper, and tension vibrated between them.

His words abruptly reminded Rebecca of the last time they'd waltzed together and how it felt to be held in his arms.

The need to leave her chair, take the short two steps separating them, run her hands over the bare muscles of his chest and arms and lift her mouth to his, was nearly overwhelming. The force of emotions he raised in her was disconcerting. Rebecca decided to obey the alarm bells that were screaming caution in her brain.

"I will—if you're there." Which was as noncommittal as she could be without refusing him outright. She stood, tucking the length of sheet more securely around her. "And since it sounds as if it's going to be a long day tomorrow, I think I'll try to get to sleep." She turned toward the screen door, hesitating to say a soft good-night before she pulled open the door.

"Good night." His voice was hushed, quieter than usual, but it still sent shivers up her spine.

Morning arrived with the promise of another hot day. Rebecca left the ranch early, well before noon when Jackson's crew was planning to quit work for the day and head for town. Colson's Main Street was crowded; following Victoria's directions, Rebecca parked her rental car at Nikki Bowdrie's Aunt Cora's home, left her dress for the dance hanging just inside the unlocked utility room at the back of the house and walked the few blocks to the city park where the celebration was to be held.

At barely 11:00 a.m., the temperature was already in the eighties. Anticipating the heat, Rebecca had donned a short, gathered skirt in bright crimson, with a white cotton tank top that barely reached the waistband. Her legs were bare and the Mexican huarache sandals she wore were her most comfortable shoes. The cotton tote bag she carried was the same crimson as her skirt, with white embroidered daisies scattered over the surface. Her hair was caught up in a ponytail to keep the heavy mane off her nape in an attempt to fend off the heat while dark glasses shielded her eyes.

The grassy park was already crowded with family groups staking out picnic areas beneath the shade of the huge old maple trees that dotted the wide lawns. Sawhorse barriers blocked vehicle traffic from the streets of the three blocks between the park and the county fairgrounds, and strolling pedestrians crowded the wide avenues. A long white tent, the sides rolled up and tied to reveal the rows of tables and chairs inside, was set up at the far end of the park, and the mouthwatering smell of roasting beef drifted out of the tent and across the park to tantalize the crowd.

Rebecca strolled through the park, enjoying the sight of toddlers with balloons tied to their wrists, children racing in and out of the groups of people with cotton candy and toys, white-haired grandmothers walking with teenagers. At last, she spied Victoria's distinctive silvery blond hair and made her way around a group of chattering middle-age women to reach her.

"Rebecca, here you are!" Victoria caught her arm and drew her into a circle of men, women and children beneath one of the shady trees. "I want you to meet Quinn. Honey, this is my friend Rebecca, she's working out at the Rand Ranch."

Rebecca instantly recognized Victoria's husband from the photo she'd seen. His black hair and green eyes were so distinctive that it would be difficult not to know who he was. He was a big man, well over six feet.

"Hello, Rebecca, it's nice to meet you."

"And it's a pleasure to meet you, as well, Quinn. Victoria has told me so much about her family, I feel as if I already know you." Rebecca returned his welcoming smile and felt her hand engulfed in Quinn's much larger one, his grip firm.

He released her and bent to sweep up his daughter, balancing her on one arm. "And this is Sarah. Can you say hello to Rebecca, honey."

The little girl shyly ducked her head against her daddy's shoulder and murmured a soft greeting. Quinn grinned at Rebecca and shrugged. "She's quiet around new people but you should hear her at home."

"She's a regular chatterbox," Victoria put in. She

touched Rebecca's arm. "I want you to meet my brother-in-law and his family."

Although Rebecca had seen a photo of Cully, still she was surprised at how much he looked like his brother, Quinn. Both shared the coal-black hair and vivid green eyes, and both were over six feet tall, their bodies muscled and powerful.

After spending an hour with the family, however, Rebecca realized that Quinn was the more sober brother, while Cully teased his little sister and was slightly more talkative. She was sitting on the blanket, trying to coax Sarah to perch on her lap, when an older woman joined their group.

"Hi, Becky. I wondered when you'd get here." Victoria immediately unfolded a lawn chair and urged Becky to sit.

"I had to finish a few chores at home before I drove in." White-haired Becky Sprackett settled in the chair and exchanged greetings with the rest of the group before her attention turned to Rebecca. "Hello there, which side of the family do you belong to?"

Rebecca laughed. "Neither, I'm afraid. I'm a friend and business associate of Victoria's, and she was kind enough to ask me to join all of you today."

"Hmmm." Becky's bright blue gaze sharpened. "You look familiar, are you sure we haven't met before?"

"I don't think so." Rebecca was distracted by Quinn as he bent to pick up Sarah. The little girl's skirt caught on the edge of a wicker picnic basket, and Rebecca leaned forward to untangle it. For a moment, the three of them, Quinn, Sarah and Rebecca, were close enough to touch. Then Rebecca freed Sarah's pink cotton skirt and Quinn lifted her, smiling his thanks before carrying his daughter off to the water fountain. Rebecca turned back to Becky and found her shrewd gaze fastened on her.

"Is something wrong?" she asked, wondering at the shock and speculation on the elderly woman's features.

"No, not at all." Becky pointed a gnarled finger at the stack of folded lawn chairs just beyond the blanket's edge. "Why don't you fetch a chair and come sit by me. I'll fill you in on all the gossip about the folks wandering around."

Rebecca laughed at the twinkle in Becky's eyes. She unfolded her legs and stood, retrieving a chair and setting it up next to Becky's. For the next few hours, she listened to an ongoing commentary from Becky, who had lived in the Colson area all her life and seemed to know everyone that passed by. She not only knew their names and what their current status was, she also knew their parents' and grandparents' history. Rebecca was fascinated by the charming, often hilarious and sometimes sad tales the elderly woman related about her neighbors.

The group went to the food tent for a late lunch, then came back to the shade beneath the tree so Sarah could take a nap. The toddler curled up next to Victoria on the blanket and fell asleep while the adults chatted, visiting with neighbors who joined them and then moved on, the groups of people shifting and mingling throughout the afternoon. When Sarah woke, everyone walked to the fairgrounds, where Cully and Quinn won an armful of stuffed animals for the little girl and eight-year-old Angelica. By the time they returned to the park, both Sarah's and Angelica's faces were sticky from pink cotton candy.

After helping Victoria wash Sarah's face and spending a half hour pushing the girls on the swing at the playground, Rebecca took an empty chair next to Becky in a circle of women. The afternoon had eased into early evening when Rebecca caught a glimpse of the older woman who had questioned her on her first trip to Colson.

"Becky," she leaned closer, lowering her voice. "Who is that woman?"

"Where?"

"There—by the ice-cream vendor at the entrance to the park."

Becky's gaze followed Rebecca's. "Humph." Her eyes narrowed over the three women accepting ice-cream cones. "Which one?"

"The woman in the blue dress."

"That's Eileen Bowdrie."

"Bowdrie? Is she related to Quinn and Victoria?"

"Not that she'll admit." Becky's lip curled in dismissal. "She's Quinn and Cully's stepmother." Her shrewd gaze assessed Rebecca. "Why do you ask?"

"I had the strangest conversation with her on my first visit to Colson. I was leaving the cafe just as she was entering and she demanded to know who I was and what I was doing in Colson. Then she told me that my plan wouldn't work."

"What plan?"

"I have no idea. She mentioned something about my eyes and told me I'd be sorry if I stirred up a scandal."

"Well, that's interesting," Becky commented.

"I found it very bizarre. Do you suppose she mistook me for someone else? She looked at me as if she knew me, but I'm sure I've never met her before."

"It's possible that she thought you were someone she knew, or thought she knew," Becky said slowly. "I can't say that I've ever cared much for Eileen, but she's had a few rough years. Of course, a lot of the problems she has were caused by her own spitefulness. And she made life hell for Quinn and Cully for years, so I'm thinking that maybe she deserved a few hard knocks."

"She made life difficult for Quinn and Cully?"

"Yes. She was married to Charlie Bowdrie when he had an affair and fathered the boys. Then their mother disappeared and left the boys with him. Gossip has it that Charlie told Eileen that he was keeping the boys and if she didn't like it, she could leave. She stayed, but she's always hated Quinn and Cully and was dirt-mean to them while they were growing up. She still uses every opportunity to give them a bad time, although there's rarely anything she can harass them about now that they're grown and married.''

''It's too bad that she took out her anger at her husband on the children. Surely it wasn't their fault that he had an affair.''

''Not to a reasonable person, but Eileen is just not rational when it comes to Charlie's kids. And then there was the will he left, which only made things worse.''

''Really? How?'' Rebecca was intrigued by Becky's recital of the local human-interest drama. Her sympathies were firmly on the side of the children Quinn and Cully had once been. Although, she thought as she looked at the two men, seated with their wives and children on the blankets spread beneath the tree, surrounded by friends, it appeared that they had survived very well.

''Clearly, the will anticipated that Charlie had fathered more children than Quinn and Cully, because it stipulated that any child that could prove parentage would receive a percentage of his estate. And he left a very big inheritance.''

''My goodness.'' Colson seemed like such a quiet town, Rebecca thought. Who knew it was such a hotbed of family secrets?

''That part of the will became public knowledge

because Eileen sued the boys over the division of property. Charlie left her an income and the house in town, but he left Quinn and Cully everything else— the ranch, investments, etcetera. She lost, of course, but after the trial, every woman with a black-haired, green-eyed child started coming out of the woodwork, claiming that their kid was a Bowdrie. It was a real circus for a while. It's settled down in the last year, though.''

Startled, Rebecca stared at Becky, taken aback. ''Black hair and green eyes? Do you suppose that's why she was so upset with me—because I happen to have black hair and green eyes?''

Becky nodded. ''That would be my guess.''

''Oh, for heaven's sake.'' Rebecca was annoyed. ''Does she accuse every person who happens to visit Colson of being her husband's love child?''

Becky laughed out loud. ''I don't know, but it seems she did with you.''

''That's ridiculous.''

''Of course,'' Becky said comfortably. ''I'm sure your parents would get quite a chuckle out of the situation. You were most likely born in San Francisco, weren't you, far away from Colson?''

''Actually, it was Los Angeles because that's where my mother was living at the time. But it was a long way from Montana.''

''Los Angeles? I thought Victoria mentioned that you're from San Francisco?''

"I've lived in San Francisco for most of my life. My stepfather owned Bay Investments and I went to work there after college. He passed away a few years ago, and now my mother runs the company."

"Ah," Becky nodded. "And do you have lots of brothers and sisters in addition to your mother... I'm sorry, I'm sure that Victoria told me your mother's name, but at my age my memory isn't as good as it used to be."

"My mom's name is Kathleen, Kathleen Wallingford." Rebecca smiled fondly. "As much as I like the name Rebecca, I always wished she'd given me her name as my middle name instead of Parrish, because I love the name Kathleen."

"Kathleen is a lovely name, but I'm partial to Rebecca myself." Becky's voice sounded oddly constricted.

Concerned, Rebecca searched her expression, but she seemed fine and, in fact, coughed and cleared her throat. Relieved, Rebecca smiled. "I don't mind being named Rebecca, but I've always thought the name Kathleen sounded elegant."

Their discussion of the relative appeal of names was sidetracked when they were interrupted by Angelica leading Sarah by the hand, followed by Victoria and Nikki.

"Rebecca, we're going to Aunt Cora's house to tuck the girls into bed, then shower and change before the dance. Becky, why don't you come with us." Victoria picked up Sarah and balanced the tired toddler on her hip.

"I'd love to, I'll have a cup of tea with Cora and visit for a while before I head for home." Becky rose from her chair and, within a few moments, the women left the park in a group, the men choosing to meet them at the fairgrounds dance pavilion when they returned.

By the time Rebecca, Victoria and Nikki walked back to the fairgrounds, dusk had fallen and the streetlights glowed. They joined a host of other townspeople, heading for the brightly lit large building just beyond the carnival midway.

"Victoria. Over here." Quinn's deep voice reached them above the crowd's chatter and the live music that poured out of the open double-door entry. "Cully's inside, holding a table for us."

The big room was packed, the dance floor already filled with circling couples. Quinn led them around the edge of the room to a table on the far side.

"Here we are, honey." Nikki dropped into the chair next to Cully and kissed his cheek.

"About damn time." He grinned and returned the kiss, then grabbed her hand. "Let's dance."

For the next hour, the group at the table shifted and changed, joined by friends who stopped to chat, then left to dance and mingle. Rebecca danced several times and, to her amazement, she remembered most of the steps to the country swing that Jackson had taught her.

Despite the socializing, however, she glanced often at the doorway, unconsciously looking for Jackson and wondering if he would appear.

When he finally did arrive, she was stunned by the swift lurch of her heart. He stepped inside the room and paused, his gaze searching the crowd without finding her. Then he moved to his left along the edge of the dance floor, clearly looking for someone. Rebecca thought she had maybe ten minutes, max, before he found her.

If it's really me he's looking for, she thought.

The possibility that he might be looking for another woman left her feeling uncertain and oddly vulnerable. She toyed with her glass of white wine and followed his progress around the room as he drew nearer, sometimes losing sight of him in the crowd.

The moment his gaze found her, Rebecca lost all doubt that he might have been looking for someone else. The instant flare of recognition was accompanied by a heat that was just as quickly banked as he walked toward her and stopped.

"Evening." He nodded at Victoria and Quinn, sitting next to her.

"Rand." Quinn's acknowledgment was abrupt and, while not hostile, his tone wasn't openly friendly, and the slight tension in the air between the two men was palpable.

"Hello, Jackson." Victoria's greeting was accompanied by a smile, and Rebecca was sure she saw the blonde nudge her husband.

"Good evening, Victoria." Jackson's greeting was polite but reserved, his expression neutral when he turned to Rebecca. "Would you like to dance?"

"Yes." Rebecca stood and laid her hand in Jackson's outstretched palm, nerve ends shivering with reaction as his hand closed possessively around hers and he drew her onto the dance floor until they were surrounded by couples.

Chapter Six

"What was that all about?" she asked, studying his face as he turned her in his arms, her steps automatically following his.

"What was what all about?" he asked, looking down at her.

"That thing with Quinn? The two of you acted as if you're feuding."

"We're not feuding," Jackson denied. "I don't have any quarrel with Quinn, but I've had a few run-ins with his brother, Cully."

"Really?" She tilted her head back and looked up at him, searching his expression. "What about?"

"My ranch shares a property line with Cully's

place. Some of my cattle broke through the fence a few times and drifted into his pastures. He wasn't happy and we had a few words over it.''

''Oh.'' Rebecca had the feeling that there was more to the incident than Jackson was saying, but he didn't seem inclined to explain further. ''Did you finish all the chores on your list?''

He shook his head. ''No, but that list seems to be never-ending. I'm beginning to think I'll never finish.''

''And did you reach Colson in time to visit the barbecue tent?''

''Yes, ma'am, I did.'' He grinned at her. ''It was excellent. But there weren't any chocolate brownies, so I settled for chocolate cake.''

''Hmm, I'm sensing a pattern here. Let me guess, you and Hank share a soft spot for chocolate?''

''You could say that,'' Jackson said dryly. ''Or maybe it's just that I've been around Hank too long and he's corrupted me.''

The upbeat song ended and a new one began, the ballad slower this time. Jackson's arms tightened, drawing her closer, his chin against her temple, her lips a breath away from the strong column of his neck. Rebecca was swamped by the same flood of emotion and longing that she'd felt the last time they'd danced like this.

''Jackson…'' Her voice trailed off. Rebecca's first

inclination was to be frank, but she was uncertain if she should admit to the way he made her feel.

"Yeah?"

The husky growl convinced her that she wasn't the only one slammed with attraction.

"I'm not sure we should be..."

He tipped his head back and looked down at her. "You're not sure we should be what? Dancing?"

"Yes." The dim light on the dance floor made it difficult to read his eyes, even though there were only inches between them. But with his arms around her, her breasts pressed against his chest as they swayed to the music, Rebecca could feel the tension that tautened his muscles and vibrated in the air around them.

For a long moment, he didn't answer. When he spoke at last, his tone was mild, in stark contrast to his body language. "And why is that?"

"Because I'm engaged to someone else and I shouldn't be doing this."

Jackson stared down at her for a long moment, his eyes narrowed. Then he stopped dancing, grabbed her hand and walked off the floor.

Rebecca had little choice but to go with him unless she wanted to cause a scene. He shouldered his way through the crowd and pushed open an exit door, taking her with him out into the night. The door closed behind them, shutting out the light and the noisy throng, leaving them in the relative darkness and isolation at the rear of the dance hall. Before Rebecca had time to protest, Jackson backed her up against the building, planted his palms flat against the wall on either side of her shoulders and lowered his mouth to hers.

The moment his lips met hers, Rebecca knew that this was what had kept her sleepless and restless these last weeks. Dreaming about him, wondering what it would feel like when he kissed her.

The world narrowed to his mouth on hers. Rebecca kissed him back, only dimly aware that her hands closed into fists over his shirtfront to pull him nearer. She sighed with pleasure when he obeyed, the hard muscles of his chest and thighs aligning with hers, pressing her against the wall at her back. She went up on her toes in an effort to get closer, and Jackson wrapped his arms around her, one hand cupping her bottom to lift her.

Yes. Oh, yes. This was what she wanted, what she'd craved during all those long nights.

Long before she was ready, Jackson's mouth left hers, and he lifted his head just far enough to look into her eyes.

"Get rid of the fiancé." He was breathing hard, barely in control. "Before we wind up in bed together and both of us feel guilty because you cheated on him."

His words hit Rebecca like a glass of ice water thrown in her face. What was she thinking? Kissing

Jackson *was* cheating on Steven. "Oh, God," she murmured in distress. "What am I doing?"

"You're burning me alive, that's what you're doing. You've been doing it ever since you stepped onto my land. The hell of it is you want me as much as I want you and, sooner or later, we're going to have each other. That's a promise. Count on it."

Rebecca stared at him, shocked by the swift, sure knowledge that he was right, that the sensual force that drew them together was too powerful to be stopped by either of them. "No," she protested automatically, barely breathing the word.

"Yes."

"But I'm engaged to Steven."

"Don't tell me you love him. If you did, you wouldn't be thinking about going to bed with me."

"I do love him." But even as she said the words, she realized they weren't true. Steven was safe, she loved that about him. He would never rock her world nor threaten her heart, but she didn't love Steven.

"Then why the hell are you standing in the dark kissing me?" he demanded, his voice a frustrated growl.

"I don't know!" She planted her hands against his chest and pushed. For an instant, he resisted, his broad bulk solid and immovable against her palms, and then he stepped back, his body strung taut.

"Well maybe you'd better find out. And make it fast."

He yanked open the door, effectively ending the conversation. Rebecca ran a quick hand over her hair to smooth it, glanced down to make sure her dress was straight and lifted her chin. Her heart nearly stopped, then slammed into a faster, heated rhythm as she met his gaze, molten with sexual promise, before she stepped past him and into the big hall.

Neither spoke but Rebecca was vividly aware of him walking behind her, her skin prickling in reaction. They reached the table where Quinn and Victoria sat, and he pulled out a chair for her.

"Thanks for the dance, Rebecca." His eyes were once again unreadable when his gaze met hers. "Good night."

He nodded with brief politeness to Victoria and Quinn and strode away. Rebecca's troubled gaze followed him as he wound his way around the edge of the dance floor and disappeared through the double doors on the far side of the big room.

"Is everything okay?"

Victoria's voice reminded Rebecca that she wasn't alone, and she sank back in her chair, managing a smile as she ran her fingers through her hair and tucked it behind her ear. "Yes, everything's fine. Why aren't you two dancing?"

"We were, but I'm thirsty so we're sitting this one out while we wait for Cully and Nikki to come back from the bar with drinks."

Rebecca forced herself to stay at the dance for another half hour, but when Victoria announced that she was tired and ready to leave, Rebecca joined her and Quinn. They walked the few short blocks to Cora's house where she said good-night, started her car and left them. She drove into the ranch yard just behind Hank's pickup and the two entered the house, saying good-night at the top of the stairs before they entered their respective bedrooms.

In the days following the dance, Rebecca avoided Jackson. He clearly knew what she was doing, but he didn't confront her. Despite the sense that he was waiting, marking time, and that he wouldn't wait forever, she was grateful for the respite, for she was struggling to come to terms with the turmoil their kiss had stirred within her.

She'd decided to marry Steven for solid reasons, she told herself. Maybe they didn't have the searing passion she felt with Jackson, but the affection she and Steven shared was safe, secure. She and Steven had mutual friends, mutual interests, and he understood that she wanted marriage and children. On her part, she understood and accepted that part of the appeal she held for Steven was her future inheritance of Bay Investments and his guarantee of a prominent position in the company.

Was that so wrong? She didn't know. But she was no longer convinced that a marriage planned by one's head and not one's heart was the wisest choice. On the other hand, she knew that passion between a man and a woman didn't necessarily lead to marriage and a happy life. That clearly hadn't been true for her mother and her father, whoever he was.

Her thoughts went in circles, and she was no closer to clarity at the end of the week than she had been the prior weekend.

The heat wave broke in midweek, bringing cooler days with temperatures in the upper seventies and low eighties instead of the ninety-plus degrees that had made Colson swelter during the county fair.

Rebecca no longer had to limit her rides on Sadie to early mornings to avoid the heat. The Saturday following the Fourth of July celebration found her and Sadie far from the ranch buildings in late afternoon. She hadn't explored this section of the ranch before and was intrigued by the rougher terrain. Instead of rolling pastures that rose gradually upward to meet towering buttes, the land resembled the Badlands of South Dakota, crisscrossed by coulees that were deeper and rockier, becoming small canyons the farther she rode. Concerned that she might become lost in the winding, shale- and rock-walled ravines, she was about to turn back toward the ranch when she saw a saddled horse in the distance. The animal was oddly still, his head lowered, and as she watched, he shifted his hindquarters, moving in a small half circle as if he was tethered to the ground by the reins or a rope at his neck. She shaded her eyes with her hand, squinting against the brilliant, hot sunlight and saw a low mound at the horse's front hooves that appeared to be a body.

"Oh my God." Rebecca lifted Sadie into a ground-eating lope, slowing the mare when they reached a shallow coulee that separated them from the flat expanse of prairie where the riderless horse stood, ears pricked in their direction. Sadie was surefooted on the shale-covered slope, and within moments they'd descended and then climbed out. Closer now, Rebecca recognized the muscular bay quarter horse—it was Shorty, the horse that Jackson always rode, and her heart stood still. She lifted Sadie into a run, terrified that the body on the ground was Jackson.

She slowed Sadie as they neared the bay, worried that the horse might startle and step on the man at his feet. But Jackson's gelding stood firm, his dusty hide trembling, as Rebecca leaped off the mare, dropped the reins to ground-hitch her and forced herself to go slowly as she walked forward, crooning to the bay.

"Easy, Shorty. Good boy." She glanced at Jackson. He was sprawled on his back, the gelding's reins wrapped around his wrist, his fist clenched tightly over the leather. His shirt was ripped at the right shoulder, the faded blue cotton bright with crimson blood, and his eyes were closed; he was clearly unconscious. Terrified, she forced her gaze away from Jackson and concentrated on soothing the gelding. He backed away as she approached, his head jerking away from her outstretched hand and pulling the reins, yanking Jackson's hand and shifting his body against the ground.

Rebecca's voice shook. "Easy, boy, easy." She slowly shoved a hand in her jeans pocket, her fingers closing around one of the sugar cubes she'd tucked there for Sadie before leaving the house. Just as carefully, she drew it out and held out the sugar on the flat of her palm, forcing herself to stand still while she kept up a soft, soothing dialogue. The bay stopped moving and took a small step forward, stretched out his nose and lipped the cube off her hand. He quieted as she stroked his nose and accepted her hand on his bridle when she gently urged him forward another small step, easing the taut pull of the reins against Jackson's hand.

"Good boy." She tugged him inches nearer, offering him another cube and rubbing his nose to calm him. He no longer trembled and stood without moving while she slid her hands down the length of loosened reins and knelt beside Jackson. She knew that she had to free him and move the gelding safely away before she could tend to him, knew that she had to stay calm or the horse would pick up her tension. With one hand higher on the reins to keep Shorty from moving, she tried to free the reins from Jackson's fist, but his hand was clenched tight.

"Jackson," she murmured softly, so as not to alarm the horse, but firmly. "Let go of the reins. I have to move Shorty.'' He didn't respond and she tried again. ''Jackson. Listen to me.'' Her voice was purposely sharper, more forceful. ''This is Rebecca. Let go of the reins.''

Jackson muttered, the words unintelligible, but his fingers loosened and Rebecca drew a deep breath of relief, working the leather free as quickly as she could. Then she stood and led Shorty several yards away and tied him to a thick sagebrush. She knew the brush wouldn't hold the horse if he spooked, but wanted to give him more encouragement to stay than merely ground-hitching him.

Then she raced back to Jackson, dropping to her knees at his side.

''Oh, Jackson, what have you done?'' The torn shirt was soaked in blood at the shoulder and down the right front; gently, Rebecca moved aside the ripped cotton, swallowing thickly as she revealed the ugly laceration beneath, oozing bright red blood.

Pressure. I need to apply pressure with a pad to stop the bleeding. Without hesitating, she yanked her T-shirt off over her head and folded it quickly, pressing the thick pad against the wound, wincing as she thought about how much it must hurt him.

Jackson groaned and her gaze shifted from her hands holding the pad tight against his wound to his face. He opened his eyes, slitting them against the sun's hot rays.

"Rebecca?" The words were mumbled, faintly slurred. "What are you doing?"

"Trying to keep you from bleeding to death."

"Good plan." His voice was fractionally clearer. He blinked once, twice, his eyes more aware. "I passed out and fell off Shorty."

"Yes." She kept her hands on the pad, pressing it against the wound. "How did this happen?"

"One of Eli's old mama cows got me. Damned thing has horns as wide as a Texas longhorn."

"You were on the ground?" He seemed to be growing steadily less groggy, and Rebecca thought she should keep him talking.

He laughed, a brief rusty sound. "Yeah. I was riding fence and found a calf down in the breaks tangled up in old barbed wire. Looked like he'd tried to walk right through the fence. I just finished cutting the wire away when his mama showed up and charged me."

"She should have thanked you, not tried to kill you."

"That's a woman for you." He shifted and grimaced. "Are you out here on Sadie?"

"Yes."

"Got any water left?"

"Yes." She lifted his hand to the pad, laying it flat against the shirt and holding it there with her own. "Can you keep the pressure on that while I go get my saddlebag?"

"Yeah."

Rebecca worriedly assessed his face, pale under the dark tan of his skin. "I'll be right back."

He nodded and she stood, walking quickly to Sadie to untie the saddlebags and return. She dropped to her knees again and took out her thermos of water, unscrewed the top and poured the metal cup half full. Then she slipped one arm under his head and lifted him slightly so he could drink. He drained the cup, grimacing as she lowered his head gently to the ground once again.

"Why aren't you wearing a shirt?"

"I used it for the pad on your shoulder." Rebecca kept her voice very matter-of-fact, but her brain was racing, trying to decide what she should do next.

"There's an extra shirt in my saddlebag. Put it on before your skin is burned. It's over eighty degrees out here."

His low growl startled her, and she looked up from the thermos, where she'd replaced the cup. The gold gaze fixed on hers was dark with pain but lucid.

"All right." She did as he asked, rolling the sleeves and knotting the long shirttails at her waist so it didn't hang to her knees. She stopped abruptly, the knot half-tied, and looked at him. "Are you sure we don't need this to tie the pad on your shoulder?"

"No. There's a roll of duct tape in my jacket, tied behind the saddle on Shorty. We'll use that."

She finished tying the knot and loosened the jacket,

searching the pockets to find the nearly used roll of tape.

"Why in the world does a cowboy have a roll of duct tape in his pocket?" she asked, returning to kneel on his right so she could better reach his shoulder and the thick pad.

"Cowboys are always prepared. Duct tape has a million uses."

"I thought that was Boy Scouts that were always prepared," she said dryly, studying her bloody T-shirt where his hand held it against his shoulder.

"Cowboys, too." He lifted his chin to indicate the duct tape. "Hold on to the pad. I've got a knife in my pocket. You'll need it to cut the tape."

Rebecca nodded, placing her hand over his to take up the pressure when he slipped his hand away. He shoved his left hand into his jeans and pulled out a pocketknife, handing it to her.

"I'll hold the pad. Cut my shirt so you can attach the tape directly to my skin, otherwise the pad will slip. Then cut a strip of tape and start sealing the edges of the pad."

Once again, Rebecca nodded. With single-minded focus, she cut and tore away his shirt before carefully sealing the ruined T-shirt tight against his blood-smeared skin with the silver tape.

When she finished and sat back on her heels, he grunted in satisfaction.

"Now what?" She wiped her forearm across her damp forehead.

"Now I have to get aboard Shorty and make it home. There's a first-aid kit in the bathroom, and we'll need it to clean up my shoulder."

Rebecca thought he needed a doctor but prudently decided to fight that battle when they reached the ranch house. "All right, but I think we should get you on Sadie. She's calmer than your horse and probably fresher since you've been out all day and we haven't."

He grunted an assent. Rebecca quickly fetched Sadie and led her closer, tying her to sagebrush not far from Shorty to keep her from drifting off. Even a few feet farther would make it more difficult, for once Jackson got on his feet, she had to get him in the saddle as soon as possible so he didn't use up precious energy.

If I can get him in the saddle. The thought leaped unbidden into her consciousness, and she just as quickly banished it. She refused to consider what she would do if Jackson didn't have enough strength to pull himself into the saddle. He outweighed her by at least a hundred pounds, and she knew she couldn't lift him on her own. She folded the knife and shoved it and the tape roll into Jackson's saddlebag along with his jacket, then she quickly scanned the ground around Jackson to see if she'd forgotten anything. She didn't think she had.

She dropped to her knees beside him once again, and her gaze probed his. "Are you sure you can do this?"

"No. But we don't have an alternative, and I don't want to lie out here, broiling in the sun while you ride back to the house and call for help. None of the crew are working this afternoon, and it would take too long to get someone from town." He visibly gathered his strength, his body tightening. "Ready?"

She nodded and slipped her arm beneath his shoulders. He sat up, paused a moment and rolled to his knees, braced his good hand on the ground and pushed upright. Rebecca went with him, bracing him when he stood, swaying for a long moment before he took two unsteady steps forward to reach Sadie. He grabbed the saddle horn and leaned against the horse's solid bulk for a moment, gathering his strength. Then he lifted his foot to the stirrup and pulled himself into the saddle. He swayed, his face even paler, and Rebecca grabbed his waist and thigh, steadying him.

"Hold on," she ordered, willing him not to pass out again. Quickly, she untied Shorty and slipped the reins over his head, knotting them around the saddle horn. "You'd better follow us, or no grain for you tonight."

"What are you doing?"

"I'm riding with you." Rebecca scanned his face,

noting the set jaw and lines of pain. "If you start to pass out, I can hold you on."

He didn't comment; instead, he nodded his head in obvious reluctance. "If that happens, don't hold on if you can't wake me. I'm too heavy and I damn sure don't want you to hit the ground with me." He managed a wry grin. "Then we'd both be hurt and who'd get us home?"

"True." She returned his smile. "Hold on."

She grabbed Sadie's bridle and led the mare to the deep ravine where she remembered seeing a large boulder. Shorty ambled along behind them, watching with interest, ears pricked, when Rebecca climbed the rock and eased onto the saddle skirt behind Jackson.

His shirt was damp with heat, clinging to his back, his body hot against hers when she wrapped her arms around him. He lifted the reins and murmured to Sadie, and she moved out, walking home.

The trip back to the ranch house seemed to take forever. Fortunately for Rebecca, Jackson remained upright, although even Sadie's slow pace made him grit his teeth against the pain when she climbed down into and out of ravines and the motion jolted his shoulder.

Rebecca heaved a silent sigh of relief as they rode into the ranch yard, but when Jackson headed toward the back of the house, she stopped him. "I know you think I can stick a Band-Aid on your shoulder and you'll be fine, Jackson, but you really need to see a doctor.''

"I'll clean it with antiseptic and tape a bandage over it. I'll be fine.''

"Maybe you'll be fine, but I won't be." Rebecca tightened her hold, hugging him from behind in unconscious entreaty. "Please, Jackson, let me take you to the emergency room in Colson. If the doctor says you don't need stitches I'll bring you straight home, but I don't want to make that judgment call and the wound is too high on your shoulder for you to see it properly and decide. And you've lost a lot of blood. I don't know for sure, but I'm guessing that's probably why you passed out. I'm worried.''

He drew a heavy breath, expelling it slowly. His chest rose and fell beneath her hands.

"All right." His voice was reluctant. "But I'm not staying in the hospital overnight, no matter what the doctor says."

"Okay." She silently decided to leave that argument until after he'd been seen by a doctor. She'd cross that bridge when they reached it.

He reined Sadie away from the house and toward the barn, pulling her to a halt next to his truck. Rebecca slid off the mare's rump, quickly pulled open the pickup's passenger door and turned back to catch Sadie's bridle, pull the reins over her head and hold her still.

Jackson dismounted, leaning for a moment against

the mare's solid bulk. Then he straightened and walked to the truck, grabbed the upper door frame with his left hand and levered himself into the seat. Rebecca immediately released Sadie.

"Strip the saddle and bridle off her and Shorty and turn them into the corral. They'll be all right there until we get back."

Rebecca did as he asked. Every instinct urged her to jump into the truck and race to the hospital, but she knew the horses had to be taken care of. Still, she stripped the tack off the two horses in record time, closed the corral gate after making sure there was plenty of water and hay available and ran back to the truck.

Jackson was fumbling with the seat belt, unable to reach it with his left hand.

"Here, let me do that." Rebecca brushed his hand out of the way and leaned across him, her breasts pressed against his chest for a moment. She caught her breath, her gaze flying to his to find the same awareness. "Sorry," she murmured, averting her gaze and carefully pulling the seat belt across his torso. He winced. "Damn." She tried to adjust the belt, but there was no possible way it wouldn't be painfully tight against his shoulder.

"Leave it," he growled.

She obeyed, gently easing the belt back against the truck frame. Then she settled beneath the wheel, quickly secured her own seat belt and put the truck in gear.

When the nurse at Colson Memorial Hospital disappeared with Jackson into a curtained-off section of the emergency room, Rebecca dropped into a chair and started to shake. She gripped her hands tightly together, but couldn't stop the quivering that affected her entire body.

The nurse at the reception desk left her chair, dropped a coin in the soft-drink machine and crossed the room to hand her an icy bottle of orange juice. "Here, hon, drink this. It'll help."

"Thanks." Rebecca tipped the bottle and drank, the cool juice sliding down her throat. "I don't know what's wrong with me. It's hot outside. I'm not cold."

"Shock." The nurse nodded her head sagely.

"But I'm not the one that was hurt."

"No, but I'm guessing that duct taping a T-shirt over a man's torn-up shoulder isn't something you do everyday, right?"

Rebecca shuddered. "No. It's not."

"Well, there you go." The nurse pointed at the hand holding the cold drink. "There's a women's rest room just down the hall if you'd like to wash off some of that blood."

"What blood?" Rebecca's gaze followed the woman's, and she realized that her fingers were stained with rusty smears of blood. So were the rolled-up sleeves above her wrists. She looked down at the front of the shirt and realized that dark stains blotted the faded blue fabric. She swallowed around the sudden thickness in her throat. "Oh my God," she whispered, looking up at the woman. "He lost so much blood."

The woman patted her shoulder. "He's a big guy. He has a lot. Don't worry," she added comfortingly when Rebecca could only stare at her. "He'll be fine. Now why don't you go get cleaned up."

Rebecca plucked at the dried blood that stiffened the cotton. In some spots, it had soaked through the shirt and glued the material to her skin.

The nurse eyed her and clucked in sympathy. "Hold on, hon. Let me get you something to put on so you don't have to wear that shirt."

She disappeared through the wide double doors and reappeared a few moments later holding a green surgical pullover blouse.

"Here you go." She urged Rebecca to her feet, tucked the shirt into her hand and pointed her toward the rest room. "You'll feel better after you wash and change out of that stained shirt."

Rebecca nodded and went to the bathroom. Her reflection in the mirror hung over the pristine white sink was shocking. Her hair was mussed, her eyes worried and dark against skin that was unusually pale, despite the tan she'd gained since arriving in Montana. A dark smear of blood streaked the arch of one cheekbone and another shadowed her jaw. She vaguely remembered using her forearm to wipe her face and glanced down at her sleeves to find them heavily spotted with Jackson's blood.

So much blood. She fought down a wave of nausea. Despite the nurse's assurances that Jackson would be fine, she couldn't get the memory of his torn skin, oozing blood, out of her mind.

She shook her head, trying to dislodge the memory, and resolutely turned on the water spigots before grabbing a handful of paper towels. She scrubbed her face and hands until the skin tingled, then unbuttoned the shirt, her fingers clumsy against the sticky buttons. She shrugged it off and let it drop to the floor. Her arms and torso were stained with rusty-looking blotches in some places, smears in others, and she ruthlessly applied soap and water until they disappeared. Satisfied that she'd removed as much as possible, she pulled the green surgical scrub shirt over her head, raked her fingers through her tousled hair, rolled up Jackson's stained blue shirt and left the bathroom.

"Any news?" she asked the nurse at the desk.

"I'll go find out."

Once again, the nurse disappeared through the swinging double doors. Rebecca paced restlessly in front of the desk, going up on tiptoe to peer through the square windows set into the doors, but could see nothing.

At last, the nurse reappeared and held open one of the doors, smiling. ''You can come on back. The doctor is done with the stitches.''

Relieved, Rebecca hurried past her.

''He's in the second cubicle on the right.''

''Thank you.'' Rebecca returned the nurse's smile and moved quickly down the wide hallway, broken up by curtained areas. As she reached the partially drawn curtains of the second station on the right, she heard the murmur of male voices.

Jackson was lying on a gurney while a doctor in a white lab coat bent over him, applying tape to the fresh bandage on his shoulder. His ripped shirt was absent, his chest and arms a dark brown against the pristine white of the gauze and tape.

The doctor glanced up, saw Rebecca and grinned.

''Hello there. Are you Rebecca?''

''Yes.'' She stepped inside the curtain, her gaze meeting Jackson's. ''How is he?''

''We put in thirty stitches, and he's going to be stiff for a few days, but he'll be a hundred-percent recovered in a week or two.'' The doctor finished smoothing down the final piece of tape and slipped a sling over Jackson's head, adjusting his elbow and hand to keep the arm and shoulder immobile. Then he stepped to the sink to wash his hands. ''I'm going to admit him for the night,'' he said over his shoulder. ''But he can probably go home tomorrow.''

"No." Jackson was curt, his mouth a stubborn, hard line.

"No?" The doctor looked at him, pulling paper towels from the holder beside the sink and drying his hands. "You don't want to go home tomorrow?"

"I'm not staying overnight in the hospital."

"I've given you antibiotics and cleaned the wound, but that doesn't guarantee that you won't get an infection. You need to be watched tonight, and you'll have to take medication every four hours. The pain medication will make you sleep so there's no way to guarantee that you'll be awake and able to monitor your condition, let alone be sure that you take the antibiotic tablet on time. I want you in the hospital where we can monitor you."

"I'm going home."

"It isn't safe." The doctor was as determined as Jackson.

"I only had a few stitches. I've had worse injuries and worked all day. I'll be fine at home."

"Is there anyone there who can monitor you tonight?"

"No. My crew is gone to a cattle sale until late tomorrow. But I'll be fine—I'll set the alarm clock to wake me up every four hours."

Exasperated, the doctor glanced at Rebecca. "Can you stay with him if he goes home?"

Rebecca assessed the stubborn set of Jackson's jaw.

"Yes, I can. But you'll have to tell me exactly what to do. My medical knowledge is extremely limited."

"I can do that. It's not complicated but he shouldn't be doing it alone." The doctor nodded abruptly and fixed a stern gaze on Jackson. "I'll release you if you let your friend monitor you overnight."

Jackson was clearly reluctant but grateful, his gaze turbulent as it met Rebecca's. "If you insist."

"I do." The doctor took Rebecca's arm and led her outside the curtain to a desk in the far corner. "The nursing required is pretty rudimentary. Just wake him every four hours and give him medication, check for fever and if you have any concerns at all, call me." He scribbled brief nursing directions and his phone number on a prescription pad, ripped off the sheet and handed it to Rebecca. "He should be fine. I'm not anticipating any complications. Your biggest problem is going to be getting him to cooperate. He's stubborn."

Rebecca laughed, so relieved that the doctor clearly viewed Jackson's recovery without reservations that she felt lightheaded. "He certainly is."

They exchanged an understanding smile and returned to find Jackson sitting up on the gurney.

"I'm going to release you." The doctor picked up the chart and scribbled. "Into Rebecca's care. She'll be in charge of monitoring your medication and temperature tonight." He glanced up from the chart.

"I've given her instructions to wake you every four hours to assure that you take the proper medication and to check your temperature. You'll cooperate, of course."

"I'll cooperate," Jackson agreed and shifted to leave the table.

"Wait a minute." The doctor stopped him. He took a green hospital gown from a cupboard and shook it out. "Put this on until you get home."

He held the gown and Jackson slipped his left arm through the sleeve. The doctor pulled it around him and over the right shoulder and arm, trapping the sling against Jackson's midriff before loosely tying the tapes across his chest.

"The nurse at the reception desk should have the prescriptions ready for you to take home. I called the pharmacy earlier." He took Jackson's arm, holding it while Jackson slid off the gurney, not releasing him until Jackson was clearly stable and steady on his feet.

"Thanks, Doc." Jackson held out his left hand and the physician took it, grinning at him.

"You're welcome. Next time, duck when you see a cow with horns coming at you."

Jackson's mouth quirked. "That's a promise. If I'd seen this one, I would have run like hell."

"Thank you, Doctor," Rebecca added.

"No problem. Don't hesitate to call if you have any concerns."

"I won't."

By the time Rebecca and Jackson left the E.R., stopped at the nurse's station to collect the prescription bottles, then walked to the truck and climbed in, Jackson was clearly feeling the effects of the pain pill the doctor had insisted he take before leaving.

"Are you feeling all right?"

"Fine. Just fine."

Rebecca eyed his slightly dilated pupils and the lazy, slumberous half-closed eyelids.

"Any pain?"

"Nope. None. Whatever is in that little pill makes me feel like I drank a half bottle of Jack Daniels."

"Ohhhhkay." Rebecca leaned across him to reach the shoulder strap for the seat belt, carefully tugging it across his torso and locking it into place before easing it snugly against his shoulder.

"How's that? Feel okay?"

"I don't feel a thing."

She hid a grin. *I just bet you don't.* "Good. No pain is a good thing. Let's get you home before the pill wears off."

He leaned his head back against the headrest and closed his eyes, staying that way until Rebecca pulled the truck into the ranch yard and turned off the engine. He opened his eyes and looked around. "We're home already?"

"Yes." She released her seat belt and his.

By the time she reached the passenger door, Jackson was out of the truck. He waved her ahead of him toward the gate, and Rebecca chose not to argue with him, looking over her shoulder to assess his walking. He occasionally wavered, but no more than if he'd had a little too much to drink, and he showed no signs of faintness.

Nevertheless, she was immensely relieved when they entered the house and Jackson turned toward the stairs.

"I think I'll lie down for a while until this pill wears off." He started up the stairs.

"Good idea." *Thank God,* she thought with relief. She'd worried that he would refuse to rest, but the pain pill apparently sapped his energy enough to make him cooperative.

She followed him up the stairs and into his room.

"Can I help you with that?" she asked when he fumbled, left-handed, with the knotted ties holding the hospital gown together.

"Thanks."

She stepped closer, keeping her gaze on the knots in the ties as she worked them loose. The room was too warm, trapping the late-afternoon heat, and Rebecca was even warmer, acutely aware that only the thin cotton gown separated her fingers from his skin.

The knots slowly worked loose and she drew a deep breath. That was a mistake, for although she'd been tantalized by the scent of warm male mixed with the antiseptic odor of bandages and tape as she worked, inhaling deeply flooded her senses.

Determined not to react, she eased the gown off his shoulders, tossed it over a chair and pulled back the sheet.

''Okay, let's get you into bed.'' She lifted her gaze to his and immediately read his reaction to her words. Despite his injury, despite the numbing effect of pain-killers, the sensual heat that blazed from his eyes was unmistakable.

Chapter Seven

Rebecca felt frozen, suspended by the hot promise in his eyes. Then he lowered his lashes, subtly shifting away from her, though he didn't take a step, and released her from the spell.

She sucked in a silent, deep breath. Refusing to acknowledge the charged air that lay between them, she gestured at his boots.

"Sit down and I'll pull off your boots."

He nodded and sat. She stepped over his legs and with quick efficiency, removed his boots. When she dropped the second one on the floor at the end of the bed and turned back, he was already lying on the mattress, eyes closed. She caught his ankles and lifted his legs onto the bed, pulling up the sheet to his waist.

"Aren't you going to take off my jeans?"

His deep drawl startled her and her gaze flew to his. Unsure if he was joking, she chose to believe that he was.

"Nope," she said with a wicked grin. "A girl can only stand so much temptation and you're an injured man. I'd hate to seduce you when you're too wounded to cooperate."

The shock on his face was priceless. Then he raked a glance over her, lingering on the thrust of her breasts beneath the loose green scrub shirt. "I'd have to be dead not to cooperate, honey, and I'm not there yet."

"Go to sleep," she ordered softly, noting the droop of his eyelids and the lines of pain bracketing his mouth. "Do you need another pain pill?"

"I hate those things. They make me feel fuzzy-headed and blurry."

"I think that's what they're supposed to do. The trip home and getting upstairs to bed must have jarred your shoulder. Do you think you'll be able to sleep without taking something for the pain?"

"Probably not." He sounded disgruntled but resigned.

"I'll get some water."

Rebecca returned to the room moments later to find Jackson lying precisely as she'd left him. His eyes opened when she set the glass down on the nightstand and shook a single pill out of the prescription bottle.

He sat up, taking the tablet and tossing it down his throat before following it with water.

"Thanks." He handed the glass back to her and lay down again, closing his eyes.

She moved quietly across the room to adjust the window blinds, blocking out the late-afternoon sun, and was almost to the door when Jackson stopped her.

"Thanks for everything you've done, Rebecca." His voice was a low rumble.

"You're welcome." Her reply was just as soft. "Get some sleep."

"Uhm." He muttered an indistinguishable reply.

Rebecca stepped into the hall and looked back. Jackson lay as she'd left him, eyes closed, his brown hair mussed. The closed blinds dimmed the room slightly, the faint shadows sculpting the muscles of his chest and accenting the stark whiteness of the bandage against his shoulder. The powerful muscles of his thighs and long legs were motionless beneath the cotton sheet. His injury and the painkilling drugs had muted but didn't erase the powerful energy that was one of his strongest characteristics. Despite the stillness of his body, she doubted that he'd be a calm, quiet patient for very long. She only hoped he would sleep through the night and give his body a few hours to begin healing.

She left the door to Jackson's bedroom open, moving quietly into her bedroom to gather up a change of clothing, then to the bathroom where she showered, scrubbing her skin and hair to remove any remnants of dust and his blood. When she was dressed again, she looked in on Jackson and found him deeply asleep. She padded across the room to lay her hand across his forehead and against his cheeks, but felt no unusual heat.

Relieved, she went downstairs to warm up soup for dinner. Still uneasy after the events of the day, her stomach rebelled against anything heavier. She switched on the television set in the living room and spent the evening trying to watch a movie, but she had difficulty concentrating and frequently climbed the stairs to tiptoe into Jackson's room. She was re-assured each time, for he continued to sleep.

When she woke him to take medication late in the evening, he didn't protest, merely lifting to swallow tablets with water before falling back against the pil-lows, asleep once again.

At ten o'clock, exhausted by the long day, Rebecca climbed the stairs for bed and quietly looked in on Jackson. He slept on, having barely shifted position since late afternoon.

At least he doesn't seem to be running a fever, she thought. The doctor's instruction to monitor him for any rise in temperature allowed her to touch him without feeling guilty that she was breaking promises to her fiancé. She lingered over the task, smoothing her fingers over the hard thrust of Jackson's cheek-bones. A day's growth of beard shadowed his jaw and lower cheeks, the stubble rough against the sensitive pads of her fingertips. Unable to resist, Rebecca trailed her fingers down the strong column of his throat, pausing at the hollow where the pulse throbbed against her palm.

The muted light from the hallway barely lit the dim room, gleaming off the curve of his bare shoulder. Rebecca smoothed her palm from the base of his throat and across the satiny stretch of skin over warm muscle to cup his shoulder, then down the length of his arm to the strong bones of his hand. The complete and utter fascination he held for her was alien to her. She'd never felt this with Steven, nor with any other man.

Reluctantly, she stroked her fingertips one last time over the back of his hand where it lay against his midriff. She left both the door to Jackson's room and her own open wide so she would hear him if he woke up and needed her, set the alarm clock for 1:00 a.m. and crawled into bed. Despite her worry that she wouldn't sleep a wink, she was so tired from the adrenaline-pumped day that she fell asleep immediately.

The alarm's loud buzz woke her at one o'clock, and she fumbled for the Off button, knocking the clock over before she managed to silence it. She fell back onto the pillow, groaned, and forced her eyes half open before tossing back the sheet.

She went into the bathroom and switched on the

light, blinking at the abrupt change from dark to bright, and took antibiotics and pain tablets from the pharmacy bottles. She ran cold water into the glass she'd left there earlier, then carried the pills and water into Jackson's room.

"Jackson?" she called softly, setting the glass and tablets down on the bedside table. He didn't respond. "Jackson?" She bent over him and touched his uninjured shoulder, jolted by the swift kick of awareness that followed the touch of her fingers against sleek bare skin.

"Mmh?" His eyes opened, staring up into hers for a blank moment before recognition dawned. "Rebecca." His voice rasped, rusty.

"Time for your pills."

He sat up and raked his hair back off his forehead. "I don't want a pain pill, just give me the antibiotic."

"Are you sure?"

"Yes. My head feels like it's as big as this house and stuffed with cotton."

Rebecca laid the pain tablet on the nightstand and handed him the lone remaining pill, followed by the glass. He drained the water, the muscles of his throat moving rhythmically, before handing it back to her.

"How do you feel?"

"Like I've been run over by a truck." He tossed back the sheet and slid his legs off the mattress.

"What are you doing?"

"I'm going into the bathroom." He stood, swaying, and Rebecca grabbed him, the quick slide of her hands over his ribs making sleek muscles flex and ripple. Then he steadied and she released him, her palms tingling from the contact. She stepped back to let him pass, then walked behind him, close enough to catch him again if he wobbled. She followed him out into the hallway, halting abruptly when he stepped into the bathroom and turned to face her, his free hand holding the edge of the door. "Unless you plan to help me unbutton my jeans, you'd better stay in the hall."

"Oh." Rebecca felt her face burn. She crossed her arms, only then remembering that she wore nothing but a thin tank top and cotton pajama boxer shorts. "Don't fall."

He gave her a dark look, mixed with amusement. "Yes, Mother."

"I'm not your mother," she muttered as the door closed. She could have sworn she heard him growl, "Damned straight," under his breath.

Men. She waited. And fidgeted. She heard the toilet flush, then the sound of water at the sink. Silence. Then the rush of water as the shower came on had her shaking her head. She didn't think Jackson should be taking a shower, but wasn't sure she could stop him. And the thought of barging into the bathroom and confronting him, while he was naked and probably already wet, wasn't a viable option.

So she paced the floor, worrying. The shower shut

off. More silence. Then the door opened and Jackson stepped into the hallway, accompanied by a waft of warm, steamy, soap-scented air. A white towel was knotted around his hips, his finger-combed hair gleaming and wet, and droplets of water glistened on his unbandaged shoulder.

"For goodness sake," Rebecca grumbled as she moved past him to catch up a hand towel hanging on the bar next to the sink. She blotted moisture from his back and shoulder as he walked back into the bedroom. He turned at the edge of the bed and, using his left hand, tugged loose the knot in the towel.

Rebecca saw the white terry cloth slip and gasped, her eyes widening. Startled, she was about to spin around when the towel moved lower and she realized he wore a pair of boxer shorts under it. Her gaze lifted and she easily read the amusement in his.

"Turn around so I can wipe the water off your back or you'll get the bedsheets wet," she snapped, annoyed.

He turned, and with businesslike swipes, Rebecca dried the water droplets from his back, bending to rub the towel quickly and efficiently down each leg.

"Sit." She turned her back on him and walked to the door, flipping on the light switch and flooding the room with light.

Surprisingly, he obeyed her and was sitting on the edge of the bed when she turned. She inspected the bandage and found it barely damp at the edges.

"How did you keep your shoulder from getting wet?" she asked, curious.

"I wrapped the edge of the shower curtain around it. Got some water on the floor, but it worked."

"You're lucky you didn't slip and fall on the wet floor. You could have broken open the stitches."

"I would have survived."

"Good to know. Next time I find you lying on the prairie, bleeding, I won't worry at all." Annoyed that he was so unconcerned over what had been a traumatic day for her, she turned to leave him.

"Hey." His hand clasped her thigh, his fingers warm and faintly rough against her skin. His touch startled her and yanked her gaze up to meet his. "I didn't mean to worry you. I've had lots of injuries worse than this one. I'll be fine."

"Good. That's good," she managed to say, distracted by the subtle movement of his fingers against her skin. The feel of his hand on her sent a rush of heat through her veins. She shifted, picking up the empty glass from the nightstand and his hand fell away. "I'll just go fill this, in case you wake and want water before it's time for the next tablet."

By the time Rebecca returned with the glass of water, Jackson was in bed, the sheet pulled to his waist, his eyes closed. She set the glass on the nightstand and quietly left the room for her own bed, where she quickly fell asleep.

A loud crash woke her and she sat up in bed disoriented before she tossed back the covers and dashed into the hall. Jackson was standing in the doorway to the bathroom, his face gray with pain.

"What's wrong? Are you all right?"

"I'm fine." He walked toward her, veering into his bedroom.

"What was that noise?" She followed him, concerned. He moved slowly, like a man who'd downed too much alcohol.

"I bumped the damn shelf in the bathroom and knocked it off the wall." He dropped onto the bed and eased flat before lifting his legs onto the mattress. "I'll fix it in the morning."

Rebecca noted the careful way he shifted his injured shoulder and arm. "Maybe you should take a pain tablet."

"I already did—that's why I was in the bathroom."

"Oh. You can have two of them if your shoulder is bothering you."

"I took two."

His arm must really be hurting, she thought, if he'd taken two of the pills he hated. "Did the pain wake you?" she asked.

"Yeah. It hurts like a son-of-a..." He broke off.

She tested his forehead with the backs of her fingers. "You're warm, but I don't think you're running a fever," she murmured, concerned.

He muttered something in reply, but she couldn't understand him. She glanced at the clock. The fluorescent arms told her it was two-twenty. He wasn't due for another antibiotic tablet until five o'clock. And no more pain pills until six-twenty. She crawled back into her own bed for another couple hours of sleep.

A noise woke her. She jerked upright, disoriented, glancing wildly around the room.

What was that? She tossed back the sheet, glancing at the small alarm clock on her bedside table as she stood—3:00 a.m. She staggered into Jackson's room to check on him and just as she reached the bed, he groaned and muttered unintelligibly, shifting restlessly and kicking the sheet to the end of the bed. The abrupt movement jarred the headboard of his bed, banging it against the wall.

"Jackson? Jackson!"

He opened his eyes when she touched his arm, his expression confused but clearing quickly. "Rebecca?"

"Yes. Are you all right?"

"I'm fine." He sat up, wincing and grabbing his shoulder. "Is it time for another damned pill?"

"No, not yet. You were talking in your sleep and rolling around, the noise woke me."

He bit off a curse. "I'm sorry." His eyes narrowed. "Have you gotten any sleep at all tonight?"

"Sure."

"How much?"

"Enough."

"What time am I due for another pill?"

"A couple of hours, maybe a little more than that."

He leaned forward and squinted at the dial on his alarm clock. "Around five o'clock?"

"Yes."

"Good." One-handed, he flipped the alarm switch on the back of the clock to the On position. "Get in bed."

"What?" She was so tired she was weaving. Surely she must have misheard him.

"You look like you're ready to fall asleep standing up. I'm guessing you're so worried that something will go wrong with me that you won't let yourself sleep unless you know I'm asleep, too. So I'll stay on this side of the bed, and you'll climb in on the other on top of the sheet so we're separated if it makes you feel safer."

"I don't think I should…"

"Oh, for God's sake," he growled. "Just get in the damn bed. I'm in no shape to jump your bones."

She stared at him, unblinking. He's right, she thought. His shoulder hurts. I'm safe. She looked longingly at the pillow and bed.

Awkwardly, Jackson stretched to pull the sheet up to meet the pillow on the far side of the bed, tugged the blanket up over the sheet and then lay flat, closing his eyes. "Make up your mind. But hurry up, because if you decide to go back to your room, I'll have to haul myself out of bed and drag you back, and the pain pills have started to kick in. I'd hate to be so groggy that I fall down while I'm doing it.''

Rebecca gave in. ''Stubborn man,'' she muttered as she walked around the bed.

Jackson ignored her. ''I set my alarm clock for five.''

''Fine.'' She climbed into bed, on top of the sheet, and dragged the light blanket over her.

She woke sometime later, vaguely aware of a rhythmic, faint thumping sound beneath her ear and a sense of warm comfort. She lay still, eyes closed, luxuriating in the unaccustomed feeling and gradually growing more awake. Her pillow lifted slightly. Frowning, she opened her eyes. Instead of a white cotton pillowcase, her cheek and palm lay against skin. Tanned, satiny skin. Her gaze flicked downward and stopped on her bent knee, snugged against Jackson's sheet-covered thigh and groin. She came awake with a vengeance.

Oh, no.

She tilted her head up, her hair shifting against Jackson's chest. His eyes were still closed, but just as she hoped he might be sound asleep, he moved restlessly and she realized that his left hand was tangled in her hair, the weight of his hand and arm holding her against his chest and left shoulder.

She was practically lying on top of him, and clearly she was the one who'd snuggled against him. He was flat on his back and, except for his fingers in her hair, wasn't holding her. She, on the other hand, was draped over him and clinging like a vine.

And it felt so good she didn't want to move. But she knew she should.

Freeing herself without waking him and without jarring his injured shoulder wasn't going to be easy. Gingerly, she took her hand from his chest and slowly shifted upward. Unfortunately, the move also lifted her face to within inches of his. Jackson's lashes fluttered and she froze.

Too late. His fingers tightened in her hair, and he nudged her mouth closer just as he tipped his head slightly to bring their lips together.

His mouth opened under hers and Rebecca murmured only a faint protest before she was lost in sensation. She sank against him and his arm tightened, his hand cradling her head to hold her while his mouth plundered hers. Dazed, Rebecca vaguely knew she should stop him, but he kissed her with such slow, sensual greed that she couldn't resist. Her breasts felt swollen and achy; she shifted to press closer and her bent knee nudged Jackson's groin. He groaned, his hips lifting.

The alarm went off, the loud buzzer shattering the hot silence. Jackson's eyes opened, hot and aware, just as Rebecca lifted eyelashes that felt weighted and stared into his eyes.

Neither of them moved for a moment, their bodies

fraught with tension, each frozen by the implications of what they were doing.

Rebecca was the first to move. She jerked her mouth from his and awkwardly pushed away, wincing when the sudden movement tugged her hair, trapped by his fingers.

"Hold still." His voice was rusty, thick with arousal.

Heart pounding, she waited until he untangled her hair before she slid sideways and off the bed.

"I'm sorry." She pushed her tousled hair out of her eyes and forced herself to meet his gaze. "That was entirely my fault." She tugged down the hem of the pajama shorts and straightened the tank top with nervous fingers. "I woke up draped all over you. I'm really sorry."

"I'm not."

"Yes, well…" She broke off, hurrying around the bed to reach the alarm and silence it. She shook a tablet out of the antibiotic bottle.

Jackson sat up, taking the pill before drinking from the water glass she held out to him. He handed it back and sat, a brooding expression on his face as she replaced the glass on the nightstand and picked up the alarm clock.

"I'm resetting the alarm." She put the clock back on the nightstand before meeting his gaze. "And I'm going to my own room to sleep."

He nodded without speaking, his eyes hooded. Rebecca left the room, the spot between her shoulder blades tingling with the knowledge that he watched her go.

She climbed into her bed and pulled the sheet and light blanket over her. Outside the window, the sun was just peeking over the horizon, flooding the room with morning light. She tugged the sheet over her head and closed her eyes, too tired to figure out what had just happened in Jackson's bed.

The next morning, both Jackson and Rebecca chose to pretend their earthshaking kiss never happened. Rebecca was daily growing more convinced that she had to break her engagement to Steven, regardless of what happened between herself and Jackson. She no longer believed that a friendly business arrangement would make a good marriage.

So Jackson returned to work outside and Rebecca to her daily management of financial files; and they both returned to treating the other with a careful politeness, each aware that unresolved emotion simmered just below the surface.

They were at an impasse. Rebecca knew she couldn't move forward with Jackson until and unless she ended her engagement with Steven. It wasn't like her to waffle and hesitate over an issue. It was much more her nature to consider a problem, make a rational decision, take action and move on. But somehow, she never found the right opening during her

once-a-week telephone chats with Steven. He seemed
so far removed from her, both in physical miles and
emotional distance. His conversations about their
friends and what was once her busy life in San Francisco felt surreal, as if he were talking about someone
else and not her.

Hank, Gib and Mick provided a welcome buffer
between her and Jackson, and Rebecca kept herself
busy and away from the ranch as much as possible.
When Victoria called on Thursday of the week following Jackson's injury to invite her and the rest of
the Rand Ranch crew to an impromptu barbecue at
her home that evening, Rebecca gladly agreed. So did
Hank, Gib and Mick. At first Jackson declined, but
the other men good-naturedly harangued him until he
gave in. All five of them wouldn't fit in one vehicle,
so Jackson and Hank both drove, Rebecca quickly
accepting the old cowboy's invitation to ride with
him. The two followed Jackson's pickup, arriving just
as the men were being greeted by Victoria, with Sarah
perched on her hip.

"Hi, Rebecca," the petite blonde called as Hank
and Rebecca left the truck and approached. "You're
all just in time. Quinn's ready to put the steaks on the
grill."

"Excellent." Rebecca smiled at Sarah, who
grinned and reached out her arms. Delighted, Rebecca
caught her, tickling her under the chin and automat-

ically shifting the giggling little girl to her left hip. "And how are you, sweetheart?"

"Fine. I have a new puppy!"

The two discussed the latest addition to the Bowdrie family, a three-month-old border collie, as the entire group started down the brick walk toward the back of the house. At the barbecue pit on the far side of the lawn, Cully leaned against a picnic table, drinking a beer and talking to Quinn. Rebecca glanced over her shoulder just as Jackson recognized Cully and stiffened, his steps slowing.

She'd forgotten that Jackson and Cully had disagreed once, something about cattle and fence lines. She looked quickly at Victoria just as her friend slipped her arm through Jackson's and tugged him with her across the lawn. The other three men followed, Rebecca and Sarah bringing up the rear. By the time Rebecca joined the group at the table, she was in time to only catch the last few words of Victoria's introduction.

"...and Hank. And this is their boss, Jackson Rand. But I think you two have met already, haven't you, Cully?"

"Yeah." Cully's green eyes were piercing. "We have."

"That's right." Jackson's voice was neutral, his stance stiff. "We met last summer."

The two men eyed each other for a tense moment.

"I heard one of Eli's old cows hooked you." Quinn's deep voice broke the silence.

Jackson's gaze left Cully. "Caught me in the shoulder. It wasn't much."

"Humph," Rebecca huffed before she thought and felt her face heat when everyone looked at her. "He had thirty stitches, inside and outside."

"That's right," Jackson said mildly. "Like I said, just a scratch."

"You'll have a scar," Victoria commented.

"Probably." The men exchanged wordless glances, shrugging at the mystery of why the women would think a few stitches and the resulting scar were important.

The moment of male bonding broke the tension between Cully and Jackson and led to a tentative truce. The doorbell rang, and Victoria drew Rebecca and Sarah with her into the house, leaving the men gathered around the barbecue pit, drinking beer.

Nikki arrived, chauffeuring her Aunt Cora, Angelica and Becky Sprackett, and the four joined Victoria, Rebecca and Sarah beneath the shade of the glass patio table's big umbrella.

"I think Hank likes Aunt Cora, what do you think?" Victoria murmured to Rebecca after dinner was eaten and the small party had moved inside.

"I think you're right," Rebecca agreed, still astounded at Hank's courtly treatment of both Cora and Becky. "Maybe it's just younger women he doesn't like, do you suppose?"

Victoria shrugged. "Darned if I know, but I'm delighted."

Rebecca laughed. Victoria was nearly rubbing her hands together with glee. "You're a closet matchmaker, aren't you?"

"Goodness, no, whatever makes you think that? That reminds me." She leaned forward and pulled open the drawer in the table beside the stuffed chair where she sat. "Quinn bought me a new digital camera and I wanted to try it out tonight, so you're all going to be my models." The sleek little camera fit in the palm of her hand. "Smile, Sarah."

The little girl looked at her mother and made a face, then giggled.

"Funny child." Victoria turned the camera on Rebecca, seated next to Angelica on the sofa. "Now, you two—say cheese."

Rebecca and Angelica put their arms around each other and mugged for the camera. Victoria rolled her eyes at them and left them to cajole Cully and Nikki into posing against the far wall. Rebecca smiled, watching the small blonde grab her husband's arm and tug him across the room to join the group. Camera clicking, she took several shots and then returned to catch Rebecca and Angelica by the hand.

"Come on, everybody has to play tonight."

Protesting, Rebecca laughingly gave in, letting Victoria pose her with Cully, Quinn and Angelica. Just before Victoria finally released them, Rebecca happened to glance across the room where Hank and Gib sat around a table playing cards with Cora and Becky. She could have sworn that Becky's eyes held tears but the older woman smiled at her and turned back to the game, saying something to Gib that made him laugh.

I must be mistaken, Rebecca decided, quickly dismissing the incident as the party started to break up.

Becky Sprackett stood in the kitchen with Victoria as the pickup trucks carrying Rebecca, Jackson and the three other men drove away. The two weren't watching the disappearing taillights. However, they were staring at the stored images on the digital camera's viewing screen.

"I can't believe that after all this time and all the searches that led nowhere, that we've finally found her. It seems impossible that the mystery could be solved so easily," Victoria said.

"Believe it," Becky said, squinting through her glasses at the photo of Quinn, Cully, Angelica and Rebecca. " Look at the four of them—they're as alike as peas in a pod."

"They all have black hair and green eyes, well, all of them except Angelica, who has her mother's brown eyes. But if I hadn't received the document with Rebecca's middle name, Parrish, on it today, I would have chalked it up to coincidence."

"I suspected when we were all together on the Fourth of July. She not only has Charlie's black hair and green eyes, she has Quinn's smile. And when I asked her about her parents, she told me her mother's name is Kathleen. What's the likelihood that a girl named Rebecca Parrish Wallingford with a mother named Kathleen, and who looks so much like the rest of the Bowdries, isn't a Bowdrie herself?" Becky nodded her head with conviction. "No doubt about it. Rebecca is Quinn and Cully's missing sister."

Victoria shook her head, still stunned. "Don't tell Quinn or Cully yet, okay? I want to double-check a few facts, like her birth date." A frown pleated her forehead. "After all these years of searching, why would her mother send her back to us? I'm sure Rebecca will be as shocked by the news as Quinn and Cully. I don't think any of them suspect a thing."

Becky's expression was baffled. "I don't know, Victoria. But it sounds like the only person who knows the truth about all this is Kathleen Parrish Wallingford. And she's not here to explain—not about where she's been hiding all these years, nor why she picked this particular time to send Rebecca to us." She looked thoughtful. "No question that Kathleen sent her daughter to Colson, or that she meant for Rebecca to meet her brothers. I can't help but wonder why. Why now?"

Rebecca rode Sadie early the following morning, returning to the ranch house to eat lunch with the crew. Jackson asked her about her ride and she answered calmly, but despite his casual conversation, she sensed he was waiting impatiently for her to make a choice between him and Steven. She didn't tell Jackson that she'd decided to break her engagement when she returned to San Francisco, convinced beyond any doubt that she couldn't marry Steven when she felt so deeply drawn to Jackson. But until she was ready to fall headlong into a passionate affair with Jackson, she didn't dare tell him she was free. She doubted she could resist if he simply picked her up and carried her off to bed and, although she was sure it would be wonderful, she didn't know how she'd feel the next morning. Nor the next week. And until she did, she wanted to keep Jackson at arm's length.

When the men left the house after lunch, Rebecca went to the office and booted up the computer. An hour later, she'd just finished processing financial data to a client in New York when Victoria called. Intrigued by the suppressed note of excitement in her voice, Rebecca agreed to meet her at her house within a half hour.

She parked her rental car next to Quinn and Victoria's SUV and noticed the black pickup she'd seen Cully drive was on the far side of the SUV. Curious, she knocked on the door of the two-story home, smiling when Victoria appeared almost immediately.

"Hi. What's going on?"

Victoria held the screen door wide and drew her inside. "Come into the living room. I have something very important to share."

"Pregnant women aren't supposed to pick up anything heavier than a pencil." Cully's deep voice was followed by Nikki's light laugh and Quinn's deeper chuckle just as Rebecca and Victoria reached the living-room doorway.

Rebecca smiled with delight. "Is that the surprise, Victoria? That Nikki is pregnant?"

The three immediately looked at her, Quinn and Cully quickly getting to their feet. No one spoke. All three of them stared at her, the two men's gazes intent, searching.

Rebecca's smile faded under the odd silence. She glanced uncertainly at Victoria. "I'm sorry. Did I interrupt something? I can leave…"

"No." Quinn stepped forward, his smile oddly tender as he took her arm and led her to an upholstered chair next to the sofa and urged her to sit. Victoria took a seat on the sofa next to Nikki, with Cully on the far side of his wife. Quinn half sat on the wide, rolled arm of the sofa next to Victoria, his long legs stretched out, his boots only a foot from Rebecca's much smaller sandal-clad feet.

"You tell her, Quinn," Cully said, his deep voice rough with emotion. "You're the oldest."

Rebecca looked from Cully to Quinn. "Tell me what?"

Quinn cleared his throat, glanced at Victoria, then at Rebecca. "It's difficult to know exactly how to explain, Rebecca. Maybe I should tell you a little about Cully and my parents first."

"Okay."

"Our father was Charlie Bowdrie. We lived with him and our stepmother after our mother left town and disappeared when we were quite young. Charlie passed away several years ago and, after his death, Cully and I learned that he'd hired detectives to search for our mother. Just before Victoria and I were married, the agency notified us that they had a lead to follow. They also told us that she was pregnant when she left Montana and that she gave birth to our sister in Los Angeles. Cully and I have continued to search for our sister but every lead we had turned out to be a dead end." He paused, his gaze fastened on Rebecca. "Our mother's name is Kathleen Parrish and our little sister's name is Rebecca."

Rebecca blinked, waiting for Quinn to finish his story. When he didn't continue, she glanced at the other three, but each of them had similar, expectant expressions.

"That's a coincidence," she said. "My mother's name is Kathleen. And my middle name is Parrish."

"Yes." Quinn's voice was gentle.

Realization dawned. "You don't think I'm your Rebecca?" But they did. She could read it on their faces. The hope, the expectation. "Oh, no, I'm sorry, but you've made a mistake. I couldn't possibly be your sister.''

"Why not?" Cully's voice was equally kind.

"Well, because...it's obvious, isn't it?" She shook her head. "Mom isn't from Montana. And she would have told me if I had brothers. Why would she have kept you a secret all these years?"

Quinn leaned forward, his big hand rough with calluses closing over hers where it gripped the upholstered arm of the chair. "I don't know why our mother never told you about us, nor why she never contacted us, but Charlie told us that she left him a note saying that she couldn't go on loving a married man, and that she knew he could give us a better future than she could. She didn't tell him that she was pregnant when she left. He never knew that he had a daughter somewhere."

Rebecca felt slightly nauseous. "What kind of proof do you have that I'm this person?"

Quinn quoted a date and place of birth that matched hers exactly.

Rebecca shivered. "This can't be true," she murmured, struggling to come to terms with what they were telling her. "I've always known that my birth was the result of an affair that my mother had before she married my stepfather. But she wouldn't talk about it and I stopped asking because my questions always made her cry. I think my father, whoever he was, broke her heart." She looked at the others and saw not only compassion but a deep reserve bordering on skepticism. "You don't believe me, do you? She's a wonderful mother—a great person. We've always been so close. She wouldn't lie to me about this. She wouldn't. Especially when she knows how badly I've always wanted sisters or brothers." Her voice broke.

"I know this must be a shock for you, Rebecca," Victoria said. "But please know that we couldn't be more delighted to have found you at last. All of us. And if you've always wanted sisters and brothers, you now have five ready-made siblings."

Rebecca managed a small smile. "Five of you." She stared assessingly at Quinn, then at Cully. "What made you decide that I might be your missing sister?"

"Becky recognized the resemblance at the Fourth of July picnic," Cully put in. "And when Victoria took the pictures last night and checked your birth date this morning, we—"

"Pictures?" Rebecca interrupted, her gaze meeting Victoria's.

"Yes." Victoria leaned forward and handed her a sheaf of colored photos, enlarged to eight-by-tens.

Rebecca was shocked. The top photo was of her, Quinn, Cully and Angelica. The likeness between the four of them was so sharp that it leaped off the page. The gleam of light off their blue-black hair, the green eyes, the shape of their jaw and the high cheek-bones—she and Angelica were smaller-boned, more feminine versions of the brothers.

She didn't need to look at the rest of the pictures. Her fingers shook as she handed the photos back to Victoria. "I hope you won't be upset if I tell you that I need some time to think about all this." She stood, clasping her hands together to still the quivering that started deep in her bones and threatened to shake her entire body. "I'm just a little—surprised."

Quinn, Victoria, Cully and Nikki quickly stood; Victoria threaded her fingers through Quinn's and Nikki slipped her arm through Cully's, offering silent support.

"Is there anything we can do?" Quinn asked.

"No, I…" Rebecca thrust her fingers through her hair and felt tears well up. "I just need some time," she whispered.

"Take all you need," Cully said, his voice gruff. "We've had months to get used to the idea that we had a sister. But I remember it was quite a shock when Quinn first told me about you."

The grateful smile she gave him wobbled. "Thanks."

They walked her to her car. When she'd fastened her seat belt and had her fingers on the ignition key, Quinn bent to peer in the window.

"Are you okay to drive?"

"Yes. I'll be fine."

"You'll call us? After you've had time to absorb all this?"

"Yes." She nodded. "I'll call. I promise."

"Good. That's good." He hesitated, as if to say more, then nodded and stepped back. Rebecca started the car, lifting a hand in goodbye as she drove off. She could see them in her rearview mirror, standing in a group, watching her leave.

She drove carefully, aware that she wasn't as focused as normal. Fortunately, the drive to Jackson's ranch wasn't a long one. She parked outside the fence, turned off the engine, collected her purse and walked up the sidewalk, climbing the porch steps with slow, precise steps. Just as she reached the door, it opened.

"Rebecca." Jackson held the door and she stepped over the threshold, moving toward the stairway. "Rebecca?" His hand closed over her shoulder, stopping her and turning her around to face him. "What's wrong? You're white as a sheet."

Chapter Eight

"I'm not who I think I am."

Jackson stared at her, trying to understand what she meant. Her face was pale, her eyes dark and wounded, slightly unfocused and dazed. His heart missed a beat and cold fear snaked its way up his spine. He swept a lightning glance from the top of her ebony hair to her pink-tipped toes in leather sandals, but found no sign of blood and his heart started beating again. But something was wrong.

"Honey, are you all right? Did you hit your head? Wreck your car? What happened?"

"Nothing happened. My car is fine."

"Okay, no wrecked car. Anything else? Bumps, bruises?"

"No."

Her voice trembled. Jackson eased her a step closer and gently stroked a strand of blue-black hair from her cheek, tucking it behind her ear. "What do you mean, you're not who you think you are? Who are you?"

"Victoria says I'm Quinn and Cully's sister. I'm a Bowdrie."

"What makes Victoria think you're related to the Bowdries?" None of this made sense to Jackson, but whatever Victoria had told Rebecca had clearly shocked and upset her.

"She has pictures. And my birth date matches their sister's. And their mother's name is Parrish, Kathleen Parrish. That's my mother's name, too, Jackson."

The shivers that shook her slim body grew stronger.

"Hey," he soothed, wrapping his arms around her to cuddle her close. Not only was she shaking, but her skin was slightly chilled, and he couldn't help but wonder if he should take her to the hospital emergency room. "Calm down, honey. I'm sure there's an explanation. Weird coincidences happen every day."

Rebecca shook her head, her silky hair brushing his throat and the underside of his jaw. "No. I saw the picture. We look so much alike—it must be true. But they said my mother abandoned them when they were little boys, and she never told them or my father that I existed. How can that be? Why would she do that?

I can't believe that the woman I've known all my life would do any of those things.'' Her voice was thick with bewildered tears and her words ended with a sob.

''Aw, Rebecca, honey…'' Jackson had never known what to do about feminine tears, and Rebecca's small sob made his chest hurt just below his left shoulder, right where his heart must be. He tipped her face up and brushed his thumb, then his lips, against the damp streaks on her cheeks. ''We'll fix it, sweetheart, don't cry, please.''

Her lips trembled and fresh tears welled, overflowing to trail down her cheek.

Jackson cursed softly and gently kissed her lower lip, then the corners of her mouth. Her shivers gradually quieted and the tears slowed. The soft curves of her body lay trustingly against him, her face turned up to willingly accept the soothing strokes of his mouth.

The fierce protectiveness that flooded him was new to Jackson, and it mixed with a surge of desire. His arms tightened to mold her body against the harder angles of his. His eyes half open, he watched her eyelashes drift closed as he covered her mouth with his, felt her go boneless as she gave herself up to the kiss. For one heart-stopping, lust-driven moment he considered carrying her upstairs to his room. But then she stiffened and drew away.

''I can't do this,'' she whispered, her eyes dark,

her expression tormented. "I'm still engaged to Steven."

"Why?" He shouldn't push her. She'd had one shock too many today, but the word slipped out before he could stop it, fueled by frustration.

"I don't..." She stopped. "I can't..."

Jackson waited, but she didn't say more.

"You don't love him." It wasn't a question.

"No." She bit her lip, already slightly swollen from the pressure of his.

Jackson felt a surge of elation at her admission, underlaid with the heavy pound of lust and a driving need to slowly slide his tongue over the edge of those small white teeth and the faintly swollen curve of her mouth below. "Why haven't you told him?"

"It's not the sort of news anyone should hear over the telephone. I have to tell him in person."

"That's not the only reason," he said shrewdly, studying her lowered lashes that shielded her eyes from him.

She pushed away from him and he let her go, reluctant to release her.

"That's the only one I'm willing to think about at the moment," she said, her eyes a dark emerald, roiling with emotion.

"All right, that's fair. You had a hell of a shock today." Jackson reined in the urge to press her for a decision, sensing that she was too stressed over the stunning news about her family. He dredged up a half smile and lightly tapped his forefinger under her chin. "Want me to go beat up Quinn and Cully for giving you bad news?"

"No!" Her appalled look faded quickly when his grin widened.

"Are you sure? I could probably take out your brothers, but you'd have to deal with the women."

"You're impossible." A small smile tilted her lips. "But it's sweet of you to offer."

"I'm not sweet," he growled, offended. She lifted her eyebrows and looked ready to disagree so he quickly distracted her. "What are you going to do about your new family?"

"I don't know." She ran her fingers through her hair at the temple and tucked it behind her ear. "I have to call my mother. I just can't believe what Quinn told me is true, but it's nearly impossible to deny the photo and the names that match and the birth date…" She shrugged helplessly. "I'm going to ask her for the truth."

"Will she tell you?"

"Yesterday I would have said yes, absolutely. Now…I don't know what to think."

"Use the phone in the office, if you want. I'll be outside, putting in fence posts behind the barn, if you need me."

"Thanks, Jackson."

Her smile was a little shaky. Jackson slipped his arms around her waist and hugged her comfortingly, ignoring his body's instant response. "Want me to wait until you've talked to her?" The words were muffled against her hair.

She drew a deep breath and her breasts lifted, pressing harder against his chest. He nearly groaned aloud.

"No, I'll be fine."

He forced his hands to let go of her and managed not to grab her when she stepped back.

"Hey." He caught her arm as she turned away, and she paused to look back at him in inquiry. He leaned forward and pressed a hard kiss against her soft, warm mouth. "After you talk to your mother, call the boyfriend. Sooner or later, we're going to wind up in bed, whether you've told him or not. And I don't want you to feel guilty afterward."

"Won't you feel guilty, too?"

"A month ago, I would have said yes. Right now, I want you badly enough to ignore even a wedding ring. Either get rid of the boyfriend, or I'm going to have to move out of the house and sleep in the barn. And I can't promise even that will keep me out of your bed."

She stared at him, silent for a long moment, then nodded, her eyes solemn, before she turned and walked away from him into the office, the door clicking softly shut behind her.

Jackson stared at the doorway, seconds ticking by, before he yanked his Stetson lower and left the house.

He returned to fencing, but stayed in sight of the house in case Rebecca came looking for him.

Rebecca punched in her mother's office phone number with misgivings. Just how was she going to ask her mother to explain what Quinn had told her? It was so difficult to believe that her chic, cosmopolitan mother had once been an unwed mother of three in a small ranching community in Montana. But on the other hand, she couldn't deny that Quinn and Victoria had what seemed to be irrefutable evidence that she was Charlie Bowdrie's daughter.

"Bay Investments." The voice was crisp, friendly and professional.

"Hello, Margaret, is my mother in?"

"Hello, Rebecca, how lovely to hear from you." The administrative secretary's voice warmed with affection. "No, I'm sorry, she's not. She flew to L.A. for a meeting and won't be back until tomorrow."

"Oh, that's right. She had a meeting on the proposal for the apartment complex in Pasadena, didn't she?"

"Yes, that's the one. I'm sure you can reach her on her cell phone, or I can give you the number of the hotel."

"No, thanks anyway, Margaret. I'll try to catch her tomorrow. What time do you expect her?"

"She said she'll be here in time for an appointment with the carpenter's union rep at two o'clock."

"I'll try to catch her just before two, then. Thanks, Margaret, bye."

Rebecca hung up the phone and thought for a moment. She knew how important the Pasadena project was to the company and suspected that their conversation would be upsetting for Kathleen. She didn't want to disturb her mother's concentration in the middle of vital negotiations, so she'd have to wait until tomorrow and find a way to keep busy until then.

She wished she'd reacted to Quinn's bombshell with a little more calm. *They probably think I'm unhappy to learn they're my family,* she realized with dismay. Even Jackson had referred to the possibility that she had brothers and a sister as "bad news." She'd been so shocked and stunned to learn that everything she'd thought was true about her mother and her background was a lie that she hadn't had time to express joy over her newfound family. She needed to make sure they all knew that she wasn't upset about the prospect of siblings; in fact, she was delighted.

She needed to stay busy, she reminded herself, and switched on her laptop. While she waited for it to boot up, she thought about Jackson's warning.

He's right, she admitted. Sooner or later, regardless of whether I've broken my engagement to Steven, we're going to wind up in bed together. Do I want that to happen?

Part of her responded with an instant, fervent "yes." But another part, the part that was still wary, warned her that the strength of her feelings for Jackson was outside her experience and that he had the potential to break her heart. Was she brave enough to take the chance? On the other hand, was she strong enough to walk away from what he offered, even if that turned out to be only an affair? And if she didn't want to risk her heart, shouldn't she run far and fast while she still had a choice?

Too many unknowns. Too many unanswered questions. Too much potential for heartache. She groaned. Her once quiet life had exploded with drama and mystery, and neither were qualities that she dealt with well. She liked organization and advance planning and... She sighed. Like it or not, she had to deal with whatever her mother told her about Charlie Bowdrie and Kathleen's own past, and she was running out of time with Jackson.

Resolutely, she pulled up files for the Rand Ranch and spent the afternoon concentrating on work.

Jackson interrupted her at four o'clock, entering the house through the back door and stopping to lean against the doorjamb of the office.

"Hi."

"Hi." She smiled at him. His clothes were dirty, his hair wet from having been dunked in the water trough at the barn, his damp T-shirt clinging to his shoulders and chest. His eyes were narrowed and she knew he was checking her face for any sign of tears or trauma. He looked hot, tired, infinitely dear and so mind-numbingly sexy that it was all she could do not to cross the room and throw herself at him.

"Did you talk to your mom?"

"No. She's out of the office until tomorrow. I'll call her in the afternoon."

He nodded, thrust his hand through his hair and glanced down at his clothes. "I'm on my way upstairs to shower. Hank's coming in to start dinner early, and afterward, we're going to play cards. Feel like losing some money at poker tonight?"

"In your dreams, cowboy. I hope you've got a lot of cash on you, because you're the one that's going to lose."

He smiled, a sensual quirk of his lips that had Rebecca's heart thudding a little faster, and shoved away from the doorjamb. "Get out your checkbook." He winked and left. Seconds later, she heard his boots on the stairs.

The arm's length distance they'd carefully kept between them was shrinking by the minute.

Rebecca's stomach twisted with nerves when Margaret put her call on hold the next afternoon while the secretary went to find Kathleen. She still didn't know the exact words she was going to use. Should she...

"Rebecca? How are you?" Kathleen's voice was warm and delighted. "I'm sorry I missed your call yesterday."

"Hi, Mom. I'm good. How are you? How was the trip?"

"The trip was fine and I think the Pasadena project is going to get off the ground. Very exciting. How about you? What's new in Montana?"

Rebecca drew a deep breath. "Actually, Mom, that's why I called."

"Really? Is there a glitch in the Rand Ranch project?"

"No. Everything's fine with Jackson's contract. The structural improvements are actually ahead of schedule." She paused. "I called about a conversation I had with Quinn Bowdrie yesterday."

The sharp intake on the other end of the line told Rebecca volumes. "It's true, isn't it?" she asked. "He's my brother."

"Yes."

"And my father was Charlie Bowdrie."

"Yes."

"Why haven't you told me—all those years, and you never said a word. And why did you send me here without telling me about Quinn and Cully? You purposely arranged to have me come to Colson, knowing I'd meet them, didn't you?"

"Yes, I did. I didn't tell you about Quinn and Cully before you went to Colson because I wanted you to have the opportunity to get to know them without any preconceived opinions about them, nor them about you."

"What preconceived opinions could they have had?"

Kathleen's voice was strained. "They must hate me, Rebecca. I left them with their father without explaining why, and I've never contacted them in all these years. I couldn't take the chance that you would be tainted by their opinion of me."

"That doesn't explain why I wouldn't have wanted to meet them."

"I was afraid that you would be anxious about meeting them, and that if you approached them first, that they might reject you because of me. After you had time to get to know them and for them to know you, I planned to tell you that they're your brothers. They didn't know you existed…" She broke off. "How did you find out?" The confusion in her voice carried clearly over the wire.

"They know about me. They've known for several years."

"But how…"

"Quinn said that when Charlie died, they learned that he'd had a private detective looking for you ever since you left. And three or four years ago the detective learned that you lived in Los Angeles after you left Montana and that you gave birth to a baby girl named Rebecca."

"Oh, God." Kathleen's anguish was palpable. "Charlie looked for me?"

"Yes. Until he died, evidently." Rebecca tried to

push down growing anger. "Everything you told me was a lie, wasn't it? That you grew up in Los Angeles? That I had no relatives?"

"Yes."

"How could you? I used to pray every night for a baby brother or sister when I was a little girl. You knew how badly I wanted to belong to a family."

"All little children want siblings, Rebecca. I didn't know that having a brother or sister was so important to you until you told me why you were marrying Steven."

"What does Steven have to do with this?"

"When I asked you why you'd chosen Steven, you told me that he promised to give you children, and that you wanted a calm, quiet, passionless marriage that would give you a family."

"And that surprised you?" Rebecca was incredulous. "Mother, I always knew I was illegitimate. Before I was eight, I overheard the maids gossiping. They couldn't believe you'd ever had a wild, passionate affair and had me out of wedlock. They called me your 'love child.' I didn't want that for my children. I definitely didn't want a passionate relationship with a man, not after seeing you cry when I asked you about my real father. It made much more sense to choose a marriage like you had with Harold. Friendly, with affection but no passion."

"Oh, Rebecca," Kathleen sighed. "I don't know what to tell you. I never knew you felt this way. The reasons I agreed to marry Harold were too complicated to explain when you were younger. And now that he's gone, I'm not sure that it matters.''

"I'm not confident that you're the best judge of what matters, Mother. The fact that you didn't think it mattered that I know I've had brothers since the day I was born tends to make me question your judgment in everything.''

"Rebecca, I know I've made mistakes, but...'' Kathleen protested, frustration beneath the words.

"I don't think I want to discuss this any further. Not right now,'' Rebecca said abruptly, the knots in her stomach twisting painfully tighter. "I'll call you later.''

"Rebecca, we need to...''

Rebecca gently returned the phone to its cradle.

So, it was true. She'd always known she was illegitimate, but she and her mother had formed their own family of two with tight bonds that made them each stronger. Granted, Harold had been part of their lives, but she and Kathleen were a circle of two. Kathleen wasn't just her mother, she'd also been her best friend, the person Rebecca could tell anything and whom she trusted completely.

To learn that her mother had a concealed past, that she'd lied to her, by omission if not commission, shook the foundations of Rebecca's world.

The phone rang. Rebecca let the answering machine pick up and wasn't surprised when she heard

Kathleen's voice. She didn't answer it; she wasn't ready to talk to her mother.

For the next few hours, Rebecca ignored the several messages Kathleen left on the machine. She went over and over her conversation with her mother and the brief but devastating facts that Quinn had given her. She ate dinner alone at five o'clock, for Jackson and the crew were on the far side of the ranch, inspecting and repairing fences. Hank had told her early that morning that she shouldn't wait dinner for them as he thought they'd be late. Just how late, he hadn't known for sure.

After tidying the kitchen, attempting and failing to pay attention to the six o'clock news on television and wandering aimlessly through the too-quiet house, Rebecca found herself standing on the porch, staring broodingly at the buttes in the distance.

Enough of this, she decided. She ran upstairs, changed into boots and jeans, grabbed a bottle of water, some sugar cubes and an apple from the kitchen, and headed for the barn. By seven o'clock, she'd saddled Sadie and left the barn. Action and the need to focus on Sadie distracted her from worrying endlessly about the situation with her mother.

Without conscious forethought, Rebecca purposely chose the more challenging route that took her deep into the breaks with their rocky coulees and ravines where she'd found Jackson injured days before.

* * *

It was after 8:30 p.m. when Jackson drove into the ranch yard. The house was dark, Rebecca's small rental car parked by the front gate.

He wondered if she was already asleep. Had she talked to her mother today? Was she upstairs crying in the dark bedroom?

He left Hank, Gib and Mick unloading the tools out of the back of the truck and jogged up the porch steps. The house was eerily quiet, the squeak of the screen door loud in the silence.

"Rebecca?" There was no answer and he strode up the stairs. The door to her bedroom stood slightly ajar; he pushed it wider and found the room empty, the bed neatly made, the window open to catch a faint breeze. He frowned. Where the hell was she?

The loud ringing of the telephone broke the silence and Jackson loped down the stairs, reaching the phone just as a woman's voice was leaving a message.

"Please, call me, Rebecca. I need to talk to you. I know you're…"

Jackson grabbed the receiver. "Hello."

The female voice broke off in midsentence. "Thank God. Who is this?"

"Jackson Rand."

"Jackson." The relief in her voice was palpable. "This is Kathleen Wallingford, Rebecca's mother. Is she there?"

"No." Jackson walked into the kitchen and looked

out the back door, but the yard was as empty as the house. "I just drove in, but I can't find her."

"You can't find her?" she said, concern sharpening her voice. "What do you mean you can't find her?"

"Just what I said. She's not in her room, the house is dark, and her car is parked outside, but Rebecca's not here."

"Oh, God." Fear threaded through her voice. "We talked earlier today and she was quite upset. She hung up on me and she's never done that before. Rebecca has always been very levelheaded and calm, it's not like her to react so emotionally. I've been trying to reach her all afternoon and evening and there's been no answer. And now you can't find her? I'm worried sick."

So was Jackson, but he didn't want to panic her mother. "There's probably nothing to worry about, Mrs. Wallingford. It's possible that she's out in the barn, or that someone picked her up and took her out for dinner. I'll check the outbuildings and then make a few inquiries. I'll call you back when I find her."

"Thank you so much, Jackson."

"Sure, no problem." He started to hang up when she stopped him.

"And call me if you don't find her, too, won't you? I'll be worried until I know she's safe."

"I'll call you back in a half hour—what's your number?"

She recited it and, after jotting it down, Jackson rang off and left the house. He strode past the truck and across the wide, graveled ranch yard to the barn. Hank was inside, hanging an assortment of tools on nails by the tack room door.

"Have you seen Rebecca?"

"No." Hank frowned at him. "What's wrong?"

"I don't know yet, but I can't find her. Her car's here but she's not in the house." Jackson checked the tack room and found an empty slot that should have held a saddle, bridle and blanket. "Hell."

"What?" Hank trailed him down the wide center aisle of the barn to the corral.

"Sadie's tack is missing." Jackson pulled open the thick door and stepped outside. But the mare was neither in the corral nor the small enclosed paddock beyond where Rebecca had pastured Sadie since she'd started riding daily. "Damn."

"Sadie's gone," Hank confirmed with foreboding before he spun on his heel and headed for the tack room.

"I'm going to call the Bowdries to make sure she isn't there." Jackson passed him, leaving the barn as Hank took two bridles from the wall and scooped grain from the bin. "Somebody needs to organize the search, Hank. Will you stay here and handle it?"

"I'd rather go with you," Hank protested. "But I suppose somebody has to be here. I'll saddle Shorty."

The telephone call to Quinn Bowdrie confirmed

that neither he nor Victoria had seen Rebecca that afternoon. Jackson hung up and called the sheriff's office to report her missing, then dialed Kathleen Wallingford to relay information. Knowing that Quinn would alert the other neighbors before he and Cully joined the sheriff's office in the search, Jackson collected an extra blanket, rifle and a first-aid kit, stopped in the kitchen to throw food in a pack and left the house.

Hank was waiting with Shorty, saddled and bridled; Mick and Gib were tightening cinches on their own mounts. Jackson packed the blanket, kit and food into the bags behind the saddle, shoved the rifle into its scabbard and took the reins from Hank.

"I've got the cell phone. I'll call if I find her. Mick, Gib, you do the same." He stepped aboard the quarter horse. "I'll search the breaks in the east pasture. Mick, you take the north section and you ride the south, Gib. When the Bowdries and the sheriff get here, fan them out behind us, Hank." He glanced up at the sky, where a sliver of new moon threw more shadow than light over the land. "Too damned bad we haven't got a full moon."

Hank grunted in assent and the three riders left the ranch yard, splitting off to move in opposite directions.

In San Francisco, Kathleen and Rebecca's fiancé, Steven, boarded the private jet chartered several days earlier for a scheduled business trip to New York.

Kathleen was terrified but didn't want to worry Steven so she told him only that they were making a surprise stop in Montana to visit Rebecca. Keeping the secret required that she go forward each time she telephoned the ranch for updates on the search, but the pilots took it in stride.

Rebecca was cold. Curled up on the ground with her saddle for a pillow and the rough horse blanket for a cover, she glanced at her watch, squinting to read the small dial by faint moonlight—2:00 a.m.

"I've got at least another three hours before we've got enough light to start walking," she murmured. She turned her head to look at Sadie, staked out several yards away. The mare shifted, limping on her right rear leg. Rebecca fervently hoped the horse hadn't done any permanent damage when she'd lost her footing in the slippery shale of a ravine. The mare had nearly fallen and, in an effort to save her, Rebecca had taken a tumble, leaving her bruised and shaken and bleeding from a few scratches, but nothing was broken.

She wondered what time Jackson had returned home and if he knew she was missing. It was possible that if the crew hadn't reached the ranch house until ten o'clock or later, he might have assumed she was in bed and asleep. If that happened, then no one would be searching for her until tomorrow, she thought—or today, since it was already two o'clock.

And she'd been so preoccupied with her thoughts about her mother and brothers that she wasn't sure how far from the house she and Sadie had traveled, so she had no idea how long it would take her to walk home leading the mare.

She fervently hoped that they'd reach the ranch before noon and that the temperature wouldn't hit a hundred degrees.

Shifting sideways, she pulled a rock out from beneath her hip and tossed it aside before curling up and closing her eyes.

Waking much too often, she slept little, startling upright at unfamiliar night sounds. Around 3:00 a.m., she dreamed someone was calling her name. It wasn't until Sadie nickered, waking her, that Rebecca sat up, fully awake. The mare's head was lifted, ears pricked, as she nickered again, louder this time.

"Sadie? What is it?"

"Rebecca." The shout echoed, the deep voice blessedly familiar.

She scrambled to her feet, cupping her hands around her mouth to call. "Jackson! I'm here. Jackson!"

The thud of horse's hooves was quickly followed by the dark shape of a horse and rider on the far side of the ravine. Then he disappeared, but seconds later, Shorty slid to a stop and Jackson stepped out of the saddle.

Rebecca flew into his arms, her face buried against

his chest as she hugged him tightly, her hands clench-
ing in the worn denim of his jacket.

"I've never been so glad to see anyone in my life,"
she said, dragging in the familiar scent of soap and
aftershave mixed with the faint smell of horse and
leather.

"Are you hurt?"

"No. I..."

His hand closed into a fist in her hair and he
dragged her head back, his mouth taking hers with
near violence. Heat and hunger poured out of him,
and Rebecca answered with unrestrained passion fueled by the worry and fear of the last hours.

At last, he dragged his mouth from hers and
crushed her closer. "God, you scared me. Don't ever
do this again."

"I won't." Her voice was muffled.

"What happened?"

"Sadie slipped on the shale in the ravine and hurt
her right rear leg. I fell off while trying to help her
and..."

"You fell off?" He held her away from him and
ran an assessing gaze over her. "You're hurt." He
traced a scratch on her cheek with his fingertip, a
scowl growing, his face going grim.

"Just a few scratches and bruises."

"Where? Show me."

Mutely, Rebecca eased up her T-shirt to show him
a long scratch to the left of her navel and just over a

rib, wincing when he touched it. His gaze flew to hers, reading the pain.

"You're bruised under this?"

"I suspect so, I'm definitely tender and that's the spot that connected with a rock when I fell."

"Hell." Jackson dug a cell phone out of his jacket pocket and punched in numbers. "Hank? I've got her. She seems fine but I'm going to take her into Colson and have a doctor check her out. Send a truck to meet us on the highway at Cully Bowdrie's loading pens in a half hour. It's likely to take us a little longer to get there, but I want to be sure they're waiting for us." He paused, listening. "Yeah, Sadie's lame. Send someone out to get her."

Rebecca moved away as Jackson gave Hank directions to locate the mare. She petted Sadie, crooning to the injured horse while she waited for Jackson to finish his call. Walking stretched her sore muscles, and she realized that perhaps she had more aches and bruises from the fall than she'd thought.

"Are you ready?"

Rebecca gave Sadie one last pat. "Yes."

Jackson loosely clasped her waist below the scratch she'd shown him earlier. "Any bruises here?"

"No."

"Good." He picked her up and settled her atop Shorty, then swung up behind her, reaching around her to collect the reins. "Tell me if you hurt or need to stop," he ordered.

"I will." With his arms wrapped around her, his chest at her back and his long legs aligned with hers, Rebecca was surrounded by him. Her battered body protested the jolting of the gelding's walk and, at first, she tried to brace herself against the pain of bruises and sore muscles. But Jackson's body cushioned hers and she slowly relaxed, letting him support her.

Two hours later, Jackson paced the floor of the waiting room in Colson's emergency room. He hated waiting. This must be what Rebecca had felt when he'd been the one on a gurney being stitched up, he realized. He glanced at his watch and, out of patience, strode through the double doors.

The nurse was just helping Rebecca sit up when he reached the half-open curtain.

"Is she all right?"

The same doctor that had sewn Jackson's shoulder after the cow attacked him looked at him and grinned. "You two ought to consider a group rate." When Jackson didn't smile, he shrugged. "She's going to be sore for a few days, but she's fine. No cracked ribs, but the bruises and scrapes are going to make her uncomfortable. I'll give her a prescription for pain medication, and she'll need to take it easy, but I'm releasing her."

"Good."

Raised voices sounded in the reception area outside the big room. Rebecca looked at Jackson in alarm just as the doors burst open and several people entered.

"Where is she? Rebecca?"

Rebecca's eyes rounded. "Mother?"

The curtain was pulled abruptly open to reveal a slim, dark-haired woman in a pale pink linen suit, leading a contingent of six people that included three annoyed nurses.

"Mother! What are you doing here?"

Kathleen Wallingford's anxious gaze focused only on Rebecca as she hurried around the edge of the bed. "I flew here, of course. Are you all right?" She caught Rebecca's chin in her hand and gently turned her face from side to side, searching for injuries.

"I'm fine. I fell off my horse and have a few cuts and bruises, that's all."

"You scared me to death," Kathleen scolded softly, clasping Rebecca's hands in hers.

"I can't believe you're here. How did you even know I was in trouble?" Rebecca was painfully aware of the unresolved questions that lay between them. Kathleen seemed her usual brisk self, but Rebecca saw her with a new perspective and it was disconcerting.

"I tried to call you all afternoon and finally reached Jackson last night. He'd just discovered you were missing and, as luck would have it, I had a charter flight booked for a meeting in New York tomorrow. So Steven and I left San Francisco a little early and I had the pilot detour to Montana."

"Steven?" Rebecca looked past her mother and located her fiancé standing at the end of the bed. "Hello, Steven."

"Rebecca," he smiled and eased past the nurse to reach the bed, bending to drop a light kiss on her mouth. "Darling, you gave your mother and me quite a scare."

"I...I'm sorry. As you can see, I'm perfectly fine." Rebecca's gaze left Steven's amused face to search the room. Jackson stood just outside the nearly open curtain, head bent and apparently listening as the doctor handed him a prescription bottle. But his gold eyes were narrowed and focused on Steven, and Rebecca wasn't fooled by his deceptively casual stance.

"I'm releasing you, Ms. Wallingford." The doctor interrupted Kathleen and Steven's discussion of the bruise across Rebecca's cheekbone. "Jackson has a prescription for pain medicine for you. I suggest you go home, take the medication as prescribed and sleep for twenty-four hours. By the time you wake up tomorrow, you'll feel like a new woman."

"Can't I just nap for an hour or so?" Rebecca looked at Kathleen. "My mother has to fly to New York and only has a few hours..."

"I'll reschedule the meeting," Kathleen interrupted, "and Steven and I will check into a hotel until tomorrow. To be honest, I could use a day of rest myself since I didn't sleep at all last night."

"Are you sure?"

"I'm positive." Kathleen patted Rebecca's hand and bent to brush a kiss against her forehead. "We need to talk, but it will have to wait until after you've rested." She straightened and swept the group with an assessing glance, her gaze stopping on Jackson. "You must be Jackson Rand?"

"Yes, ma'am."

Kathleen squeezed Rebecca's shoulder. "I'm assuming you'll be taking Rebecca home?"

"Just as soon as she's ready."

"Good. And we'll drive out tomorrow morning to visit her after she's awake and feeling better."

"See you tomorrow, Rebecca." Steven leaned in close and kissed her again.

The brief kiss held a definite note of ownership. Steven lifted his head and Rebecca stared at him, confused. Then his gaze flicked to the other side of the gurney, and she realized that Jackson stood there, waiting.

Rebecca was abruptly aware that Jackson was angry. His body radiated a restrained menace, his eyes were remote and a muscle flexed along his jawline. Barely restrained hostility thickened the air between the two men.

"Ready to go?"

"Yes." She started to sit up.

Jackson slipped his arms under her knees and around her back and swung her off the gurney. Startled, she instinctively slid her free arm around his neck.

"We'll call you in the morning, Mrs. Wallingford, as soon as Rebecca's awake and ready for visitors." His deep voice held no hint of the tension that strung his body as he headed for the exit.

"How will you know what hotel we're staying at?" Steven's voice followed them, faintly annoyed.

"There's only one in town." Jackson didn't turn or slow down, he just kept walking.

"I'll see you tomorrow, Mom," she said over Jackson's shoulder just as the double doors closed behind them.

She waited until he'd settled her in the truck and they were driving out of the hospital's parking lot. "I've known Steven since we were children."

He flicked her a glance, his eyes molten. "So?"

"I just wanted to explain that we've been friends for years, and he's been hugging and kissing me hello since we were kids. It doesn't mean anything."

"He didn't kiss you like a 'friend.' And you're engaged to him."

"True." Rebecca wasn't sure she wanted to confess that Steven had never kissed her possessively before.

"But you won't be after tomorrow."

The look he gave her was fierce, demanding. Rebecca swallowed, her throat dry. "No," she admitted. "I won't be engaged after tomorrow."

The swift flare of heat in his eyes stole her breath.
"Good. With luck, I'll be able to keep my hands
off you until then."

The following afternoon, Rebecca and Kathleen
sent Steven out onto the porch with a tall glass of
iced tea and retired to Rebecca's room upstairs. Rebecca curled up at the foot of the bed, and Kathleen
took a seat on the single, straight-backed chair.

"I owe you an apology, Rebecca. I should have
told you about your father, and about Quinn and
Cully. All I can say in my defense is that I truly
thought it would be easier for you if you didn't know
about them."

"I don't understand, Mom. How could it have been
better to never know I had brothers?"

Kathleen thrust her fingers through her short-
cropped dark hair and sighed. "Because there never
was any possibility that we could return here. Nor did
I think that Charlie would ever have let them visit us
in San Francisco."

"But why? Quinn said Charlie tried to find you
until the day he died. Surely that's not the action of
a man who would have forbidden your sons to see
you?"

"In retrospect, no. But I didn't know that. And I
had every reason to believe that if I left him, he'd
hate me."

"Did he tell you he'd hate you?"

"Not in so many words, no. But I knew Charlie so well. Or at least, I thought I did."

"Why did you leave him, Mom, and why did you leave the boys here?"

"I left because I loved Charlie too much to stay. And that's the same reason I didn't take the boys with me." Kathleen rose and paced to the window to stare out. "I didn't know Charlie was married when I met him. By the time he told me, I loved him too much to stop seeing him—and he felt the same about me. But he loved the family ranch more than life itself. If he'd divorced Eileen, she would have demanded half of the ranch. And losing the ranch would have broken his heart. He didn't have children with Eileen and he loved the boys so much…. I couldn't stay and go on being his mistress, but I couldn't take his sons away from him." She looked at Rebecca, deep sadness etched on her features. "I knew I was pregnant with you when I left Colson and I knew the baby was a girl. Selfishly, I didn't tell him. It broke my heart to leave my boys with Charlie. I didn't think it was too much to ask that I get to keep my little girl."

"Oh, Mom." Rebecca shook her head, not knowing what to say in the face of her mother's anguish. "Why didn't you tell me?"

"I'd always planned to—but time went by, and there never seemed to be the right moment. I told myself that you were a happy child, well adjusted, busy with friends and later with your career, and it wouldn't make a big impact on your life to learn you had brothers. Lots of your friends had half brothers and sisters, stepsiblings with whom they had little contact, and it didn't seem an important issue for them. And then you told me why you became engaged to Steven and I realized that I'd badly miscalculated. That's when I started looking for a reason to send you to Colson.''

Rebecca suddenly understood why Bay Investments had funded Jackson's expansion. ''That's why you invested in the Rand Ranch? Solely to have an excuse to send me to Colson to meet Quinn and Cully?''

''Yes. Not that it wasn't a good investment,'' Kathleen added. ''It is. But I wasn't looking to expand our business into Montana until I needed to find a way to move you into your brothers' orbit.''

''You should have told me, Mom.''

''Should I?'' Kathleen left the window and sat on the bed facing Rebecca. ''Are you sure you would have been comfortable meeting them if you'd known who they were? Can you swear, after meeting them, they wouldn't have held it against you that you lived with me while you were growing up? Been influenced by a woman they must surely resent?''

Chapter Nine

"I don't know them well enough to answer," Rebecca said. But she remembered the doubt on their faces when she told them what a wonderful person Kathleen was—would they have accepted her so readily if they'd known from their first meeting who she was? And would she have become friends with Victoria and eased into a comfortable acquaintance with Quinn and Cully if she'd known they were her brothers before she met them? "I would hope not," she added slowly. "But I'm simply not sure." Her gaze met Kathleen's. "You need to talk to them. They deserve to hear what you've told me today."

Kathleen's eyes darkened. "I know." Restless, she stood and walked to the window again, her fingers twisting the carved gold chain that matched the loops in her earlobes. "Here comes Jackson," she commented, turning to give Rebecca a wry smile. "I'm guessing that you need to talk to Steven about him?"

"Yes, I do."

"Then let's go downstairs before Jackson reaches the house. Best not to leave him alone with Steven for very long. I'll ask him to give me a tour of the ranch upgrades while you and Steven have a chat."

Rebecca stood, wincing as the movement pulled sore muscles. Kathleen slipped her arm through Rebecca's as they walked to the door.

"Am I going to have a new future son-in-law soon?" she asked.

"I don't think Jackson is the marrying kind."

"Don't be too sure," Kathleen whispered as they descended the stairs slowly in deference to Rebecca's aches and pains. "The man was giving you looks that had me searching for a fan and ice water."

"Mom!" Rebecca didn't know whether to laugh or be scandalized by her mother's easy acceptance of Jackson.

"Shhh, here they are."

Rebecca managed a smile as Jackson and Steven both greeted them, despite the swift rush of heat that burned her throat and cheeks when Jackson's gaze swept her from head to toe.

* * *

Three hours later, Rebecca stood next to Jackson on the porch and waved goodbye to her mother as Steven drove their rental car away from the house and down the lane to the highway.

"Everything cleared up with your mother?" Jackson asked, watching the cloud of dust rising behind the vehicle.

"Yes. She agrees with me that she owes Quinn and Cully an explanation of what happened and why she abandoned them all those years ago. She's going to ask them to meet with her when she returns, after the New York meetings are finished."

"That's only a week away."

"I know. I hope they'll listen and give her a chance to explain why she had to leave Colson."

Jackson nodded silently. He caught her left hand in his and lifted it, rubbing his thumb over the bare third finger. "So," he said softly. "You told the boyfriend to get lost?"

"I ended the engagement, yes." Rebecca's heart skipped a beat, stalled, then raced faster as he lifted her hand to his lips and pressed a hot, openmouthed kiss into the sensitive palm.

"There's a poker game at Joe's house tonight. Hank, Gib and Mick will probably be there until late. Very late."

"You're not playing poker at Joe's tonight?"

"No." He shook his head, a slow, sensual smile curving his lips. "I'm not playing poker tonight."

The sound of Hank's pickup engine broke the hot silence.

Rebecca pulled her hand from Jackson's and escaped into the house before she had to face the crew, convinced that they would take one look at her face and know that she planned to seduce Jackson.

She escaped upstairs for a shower after dinner and, by the time she left the bathroom and returned to her room to dress, the men were outside, teasing each other good-naturedly as they piled into Hank's truck. Doors slammed, the engine turned over, gravel crunched under truck tires as the pickup left the ranch yard and peace reigned once more.

Rebecca slipped out of her robe and pulled on a white sundress, fastening tiny buttons from midthigh to just between her breasts. She didn't bother with a bra or panties and the light cotton was cool against bare skin, shifting to gently abrade sensitive nipples and brush her thighs as she walked downstairs. The house was quiet. She peered into the living room but Jackson wasn't there, and she walked to the screen door to look out. He lounged in one of the old oak rockers on the porch, wearing only faded Levi's in the evening heat, his feet and torso bare, his head resting against the high back.

The screen door squeaked when she pushed it open, and he turned his head to look at her.

The door slapped softly shut. She felt the touch of his gaze as if he'd run his hands over her. Her nipples tightened and slow heat unfurled in her belly.

"Come here." His voice was a slow drawl, roughened with the need that lay between them. He held out his hand, and she walked to him, the painted boards of the porch floor cool beneath her feet. The setting sun's rays were warm across her bare shoulders. She knew the second he realized she was naked under the dress, for his gaze brushed over her body, lingering on her breasts and the apex of her thighs. "You're amazing. And so damned beautiful you take my breath away."

He took her hand and tugged, pulling her forward and into his lap. He brushed a strand of hair from her cheek, his eyes hooded shards of gold, intent on hers.

"Tell me you want this."

She caught her breath, seduced by the husky restraint in his voice. She brought her mouth to his, her breasts peaking beneath the thin cotton as she pressed against his bare chest. "I want you," she murmured.

"Thank God," he whispered before he threaded his fingers through her hair and took her mouth.

The kiss was hot and carnal, and went on and on until he tore his mouth from hers to abruptly stand, cradling her, and cross the porch, bending to open the screen door before climbing the stairs to his room. He set her on her feet by the bed and tugged her skirt upward. His hands on the back of her thighs had her pressing urgently against him but when he reached the bare curve of her bottom, he went still.

"You're really naked under this dress?" he murmured against her lips.

"I thought it was a waste of time to put on underclothes when I knew you'd just take them off again."

"You were right." He pulled the dress up and off over her head, letting it drop to the floor while he stared at her. "You're so damn beautiful." He brushed the back of his fingers over the slope of her breast and the ruched pink nipple, then lower across the smooth skin of her belly to the nest of black curls below.

Rebecca's eyelids drooped, heavy with arousal and the erotic touch of his hands on her. His gaze returned to hers and she knew he was done with seduction. Her heart pounded as he stripped off his jeans and wrapped her close, dropping onto the bed and rolling her under him in one swift move.

She welcomed the hot press of his body against hers, the hard thigh that nudged her knees apart, the thrust of his tongue against hers. She'd wanted this, wanted him, for what seemed like forever. And the reality was better than all her hot dreams.

"Next time we'll go slow, honey," he said as he tore open a condom and rolled it on. "I promise."

"Next time," she murmured, urging him closer,

wrapping her legs around his waist as he surged inside her, screaming when he drove them both over the edge.

A short week after Kathleen left for New York, she returned to Colson without Steven, who flew on to San Francisco. During several phone conversations, Rebecca had convinced her mother to let her arrange a meeting with Quinn and Cully.

Kathleen was pale and composed, but for a brief moment, Rebecca saw panic in her eyes when her brothers' trucks drove into the ranch yard. Rebecca pulled back the living-room curtain, and her mother stood behind her, watching as the pickups parked near the front gate and Quinn and Cully emerged.

Her sharp, indrawn breath was exhaled on a faint sob as they handed out their wives and walked toward the house.

"Are you going to be okay with this?" Rebecca asked, scanning Kathleen's pale face. She'd seen Kathleen handle hostile takeover bids and irate clients with icy calm; she'd never seen this level of trepidation on her face.

"Yes." Kathleen's slim shoulders visibly squared beneath the jacket of the pale blue linen suit, though she flinched slightly at the rap of knuckles on the screen door. Rebecca hesitated and Kathleen patted her cheek with cold fingers. "Go let them in, hon, and let's get this over with."

Rebecca knew her mother anticipated rejection, but

having seen both Quinn and Cully with their wives and children, she knew they had a deep capacity for kindness. She fervently hoped they would extend that compassion to Kathleen.

But when she pulled open the door and saw their faces, she wasn't sure she'd done the right thing in arranging this meeting. Both men's faces were grim, their eyes remote. They looked big, mean and dangerous. Her anxious gaze flicked to Victoria and Nikki. Both women smiled encouragingly.

"Come in." She held the screen door open and the four stepped past her. "Mom's in the living room."

They waited, letting her lead the way. Kathleen stood next to the large upholstered armchair, hands clasped at her waist. Her chic blue suit and matching linen pumps, gold earrings, watch and rings were a subtle statement of the woman she'd become, and Rebecca knew that the outer trappings of position and wealth were her mother's armor.

Kathleen didn't speak, nor did Quinn and Cully. They stared at each other across the expanse of hardwood floor, as if searching for some small semblance of the mother and children that each remembered.

"Mother," Rebecca said, determined to ease the difficult meeting. "This is Quinn and his wife, Victoria, and Cully and his wife, Nikki."

"Good morning," Kathleen murmured.

Emotion shadowed Quinn's face in reaction to her distinctive clear voice, but was just as quickly gone.

He nodded briefly, as did Cully, while Nikki and Victoria both said good morning.

"Shall we all sit down?" Rebecca gestured to the sofa, wishing she'd taken Jackson up on his offer to join her. She'd badly wanted to have his support, but had decided that Quinn and Cully might be more comfortable if the first meeting with their mother included as few people as possible.

Kathleen sat stiffly in the cushioned armchair, her spine a foot away from the chair back, hands clasped in her lap, ankles crossed. Victoria and Nikki sat on the sofa cushions, the two men half sitting on the wide arms, clearly too tense to settle completely.

Rebecca looked at her mother and her brothers, all three tense and clearly uncomfortable, then at Victoria and Nikki. Both women nodded encouragingly. She decided to skip any attempts at polite conversation and cut straight to the chase.

"If no one has any objections, I think Mom should tell us what happened thirty-some years ago. That might answer many questions more quickly."

"Sounds good." Quinn's deep voice was neutral. Cully only nodded. Both men focused intently on Kathleen.

"Very well." She hesitated, as if collecting her thoughts. When she spoke, her voice was calm, as if she were telling someone else's story and not her own. "I met Charlie Bowdrie when I was seventeen. I worked weekends at a restaurant, waiting tables to save money for college. He was a regular and came in several times a week for lunch or dinner. He didn't tell me he was married and, since I lived in Wolf Point and not in Colson, I had no way of knowing. He took me to dinner and a movie on my eighteenth birthday, and we saw each other several times a week after that. I became pregnant that summer and assumed we'd marry. He told me he loved me, but he couldn't marry me. He was already married.'' For a moment, emotion flickered across the calm planes of Kathleen's face, and her voice faltered. But then she rallied and continued speaking. "I lived with my aunt, my mother's sister, and she was furious when she learned I was pregnant. She was even angrier when I refused to have an abortion. She disowned me and threw me out. When Charlie found out, he rented a house and insisted that I move in. I'd stopped seeing him when I found out he was married, but I was all alone and the pregnancy was difficult. By the time the baby was born, Charlie was spending a lot of time at the house and he adored you, Quinn. He loved being a father and his wife couldn't have children.'' Her gaze met Quinn's, then moved to Cully. "And then you were born, Cully, and he loved you just as much. You boys were the reason he lived and breathed— you two, and the Bowdrie Ranch.'' She paused. "He would have divorced Eileen and married me, I believe, if it hadn't been for the ranch.''

"What do you mean?" Cully's voice was as deep as Quinn's and just as devoid of emotion.

"Had they divorced, she was entitled to fifty percent of the assets. She would have forced him to sell the ranch and give her half the proceeds. She wouldn't agree to leave the ranch intact and accept half the income. She demanded cash."

Kathleen brushed a wisp of hair behind her ear in a small gesture that betrayed fraught nerves. "I loved Charlie but I struggled with the morality issue. He told me he wasn't happy with Eileen, but I couldn't reconcile myself to life as the 'other woman.' I suspected that I was pregnant again the day that Eileen came to see me."

Rebecca stiffened. Kathleen had already told her most of the story, but not that Eileen had sought her out.

"She told me that she knew her marriage to Charlie could be saved if I were out of the picture. When I told her that Charlie would never be happy without his children and no matter how far I ran, he'd follow to reclaim them, she cried and told me that she was unable to conceive, but that she longed to be a mother and that she would give my boys a good home. She swore she would accept my children as her own, and that Quinn and Cully would be Charlie's heirs, that they would have a respectable place in the community and a bright, solid future."

Quinn and Cully voiced twin growls of derision.

Kathleén paused, stiffening before continuing, her voice nearly devoid of expression, as if she were reciting from a textbook. "The following day, I learned I was pregnant. Three days later, I left town. And I left you boys with your father."

"Where did you go?" Victoria's voice was warm with sympathy.

"I took the first bus out of town. It happened to be going east and I got as far as Chicago before I changed to a bus heading south. Looking back, I don't think I was very coherent during those first few days. When the bus I was riding stopped at a station, I'd get off and then board the next one leaving—I didn't really care what its destination was. I zigzagged across the midwest and south, then west, before I landed in Los Angeles. I liked the Pacific Ocean, so I stayed."

"No wonder the detective couldn't trace you," Quinn commented.

"How long were you in Los Angeles? That's where I was born, correct?" Rebecca asked.

"Yes, you were born in L.A., but we didn't stay there long. I had a job as a maid for a Belize family connected to the embassy. They returned to Belize and I went with them."

"And that's where you met Harold." Rebecca had heard this part of the story, but wondered how much of what she'd been told was true.

"Yes. The family had a home in Belize City and

another in the country. Harold was a guest of the family, along with several other friends, at a house party in the country house. When guerrilla bandits attacked the house, they killed several of the guests and marched the rest of us into the hills where they held us for ransom.''

"Oh, Mom." Rebecca was stunned.

"I wasn't worth anything to them. They would have shot us both if they'd known I was penniless, but Harold told them I was his wife and you were his daughter and that he would arrange ransom money for all of us. It was weeks before the money was transferred and, by then, the guerrillas had moved us repeatedly. They released us in Colombia, and in order to get us all out of the country without passports, Harold also told the authorities that we were married and you were our child. We flew back to the States and, after a year, I married Harold and you took his name.''

"So that's why I lost the trail in Belize," Cully said to Quinn.

"You were in Belize?" Kathleen looked stunned.

"Yes. Several years ago."

"Looking for us?"

"Looking for Rebecca," he corrected.

"Oh." Kathleen paled. "The rest of the story, you already know. I remained in San Francisco and built a life for myself and Rebecca. I didn't contact Charlie, nor you boys. That was part of the bargain I'd made with Eileen. It wasn't until Rebecca told me that she planned to marry a friend, so that she could have children and the family she'd always craved, that I realized I'd made a very bad decision in not telling her about you.''

"So you admit that you purposely sent Rebecca to Colson?'' Quinn asked.

"Yes. I sent her here to meet you both.'' She drew a deep breath. "I know you and Cully have cause to hate me, Quinn, but I pray you won't reject Rebecca for my sins. All I can say in my own defense is that I was very young when I made the decision to leave you with your father. It broke my heart, and not a day went by that I didn't agonize over whether I'd done the right thing. But once done, there was no going back.'' Once again, she firmed her chin, clearly bracing herself for a blow.

On the sofa, Victoria slipped her hand into Quinn's. Nikki did the same with Cully, and both men exchanged glances with their wives.

Rebecca held her breath, tears blurring her vision after hearing Kathleen's heart-wrenching story. Both Quinn and Cully looked at her, their faces softening slightly, before their identical emerald gazes moved to Kathleen.

"I can't say that I think you made the right choice.'' Quinn's voice held no rancor. "But I'm trying to imagine Victoria in your situation, and it's hard to believe she would deserve to be punished for the rest of her life. Especially when it doesn't sound as if there was any way for everyone to be happy.''

"If Eileen hadn't lied through her teeth, or if she hadn't been the stepmother from hell, the story might have had a happier conclusion,'' Cully commented. ''Too bad her intentions weren't as well-meaning as yours.''

Kathleen couldn't speak. Tears welled and slowly overflowed to ease down her cheeks. She looked helplessly at Rebecca, who wiped away her own tears.

"On that note, I think we should adjourn to the kitchen for coffee and cake. I couldn't eat a thing this morning and I'm starving.''

Her comments eased the awkward, emotion-filled moment, and the group rose to troop into the kitchen. Rebecca knew that, despite the difficult years of separation that lay between them, her mother and brothers were open to healing the breach. She didn't know just how long it might take for Kathleen to build a relationship with Quinn and Cully, but she was relieved and elated that her brothers hadn't rejected her mother's appeal out of hand.

During the next few days, Kathleen met Quinn's daughter, Sarah, and Angelica, who was openly curious about her half sister's mother. When the little girl declared Kathleen an official grandmother, the adults were charmed and smiled indulgently. Kathleen and her sons moved more slowly toward acceptance, but all three were obviously trying to ease the awkwardness.

Kathleen had to return to San Francisco after only four days due to work demands, but in the following weeks, she flew to Colson several times to visit.

During one of her visits, Jackson and Rebecca drove into Colson to meet her, Quinn, Victoria and Sarah, Cully, Nikki and Angelica, for lunch.

Hand in hand, Angelica and Sarah skipped ahead beside Kathleen, reaching the entrance to the cafe just as the door opened.

Eileen Bowdrie stepped out onto the sidewalk and stopped dead, staring at Kathleen.

Rebecca's fingers gripped Jackson's. "Oh, no," she breathed.

"What's wrong?" His gaze followed hers and he bit off a curse.

"I can't believe you have the nerve to show your face in Colson." Eileen's voice quivered with anger and her pale face flushed, eyes narrowing.

"Hello, Eileen." Kathleen's voice was calm.

"What are you doing here?" the other woman demanded.

"I'm visiting my children."

The oddly gentle, simple answer was as effective as a slap in the face. Eileen's gaze moved past her to Quinn and Victoria, Cully and Nikki, Rebecca and Jackson, ranged in a protective semicircle behind

Kathleen. Emotions moved quickly across Eileen's face, reflecting a mix of anger, regret and pain.

Without another word, Eileen slipped on designer sunglasses to conceal her eyes and turned on her heel to move stiffly away down the sidewalk, a solitary figure in an expensive silk dress and gold jewelry.

Rebecca drew a sigh of relief, though she thought the woman's abrupt departure was odd. One glance at Kathleen reassured her, for her mother was chatting easily with Angelica and asking her to take Sarah's hand to enter the cafe.

"I feel sorry for her," Jackson commented, staring after Eileen as the group slowly moved ahead of them into the air-conditioned cafe.

"For Eileen?" Rebecca's gaze followed his, and she frowned. "Why would you..."

"Hey, you two, hurry up." Victoria called, holding the door open.

It wasn't until later that night, when she was curled next to Jackson in the comfort of his bed, that Rebecca found time to ask him what he'd meant at the cafe.

"Tell me why you felt sorry for Eileen Bowdrie, Jackson. After all of the trouble she's caused for my family, I can't believe that you'd feel sorry for her."

Jackson smoothed his hand over the bare curve of her breast, his fingers lingering to test the silky skin. "Because after all these years, she has no husband

and no children—no one who loves her. She's all alone. That's a terrible place to be, Rebecca, without a soul in the world who cares what happens to you. I've been there. I know what it's like."

Struck by his perception, Rebecca hugged him fiercely. "But you're not there now, Jackson, and you'll never be again, because I love you."

"Yeah?" Jackson's voice was rough.

"Yes."

"Then marry me."

Rebecca froze. "Marry you?" she repeated carefully.

"Yeah, marry me. I don't ever want to be without you again."

"I don't want to live without you, either, Jackson." Her smile was misty.

"I don't know how we'll work out your job in California and my work here, but we'll find a way."

"Okay. And we'll have children, at least one little girl and a little boy?"

"As many as you want," Jackson promised.

"Maybe we could have one of each and see how it goes?"

"Sounds like a good plan."

"You're going to make such a good father." She hugged him. "I love you so much."

"I love you, too, sweetheart. I never thought it was in the cards that I'd love anyone like this, or that any woman would ever love me the way you do. Now I think maybe anything's possible, a family of my own, children to love, all because you love me. It's a damned miracle.''

''Oh, Jackson.'' Rebecca's voice wavered, her eyes misty with tears.

''You're not crying, are you?''

''No.''

''Good.'' He kissed her with fierce possession and, just before Rebecca lost all ability to think of anything but him, she realized that she, too, had found all that she'd once thought she'd never have. All because Jackson loved her.

*   *   *   *   *

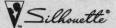